Here Lies The Body

Books by Scott Corbett

Suspense Stories

TREE HOUSE ISLAND
DEAD MAN'S LIGHT
CUTLASS ISLAND
ONE BY SEA
COP'S KID
THE BASEBALL BARGAIN
THE MYSTERY MAN
THE CASE OF THE GONE GOOSE
THE CASE OF THE FUGITIVE FIREBUG
THE CASE OF THE TICKLISH TOOTH
THE CASE OF THE SILVER SKULL
THE RED ROOM RIDDLE
DEAD BEFORE DOCKING
RUN FOR THE MONEY
HERE LIES THE BODY

Easy-to-Read Mysteries

DR. MERLIN'S MAGIC SHOP
THE GREAT CUSTARD PIE PANIC

The Trick Books

THE LEMONADE TRICK
THE MAILBOX TRICK
THE DISAPPEARING DOG TRICK
THE LIMERICK TRICK
THE BASEBALL TRICK
THE TURNABOUT TRICK
THE HAIRY HORROR TRICK
THE HATEFUL PLATEFUL TRICK
THE HOME RUN TRICK
THE HOCKEY TRICK

What Makes It Work?

WHAT MAKES A CAR GO?
WHAT MAKES TV WORK?
WHAT MAKES A LIGHT GO ON?
WHAT MAKES A PLANE FLY?
WHAT MAKES A BOAT FLOAT?

Here Lies The Body

SCOTT CORBETT

Illustrated by Geff Gerlach

An Atlantic Monthly Press Book
Little, Brown and Company
Boston · Toronto

FIRST EDITION

T 09/74

Library of Congress Cataloging in Publication Data

Corbett, Scott.
  Here lies the body.

  "An Atlantic Monthly Press book."
  [1. Witchcraft--Fiction] I. Title.
PZ7.C79938He   [Fic]   74-6202
ISBN 0-316-15717-1

ATLANTIC—LITTLE, BROWN BOOKS
ARE PUBLISHED BY
LITTLE, BROWN AND COMPANY
IN ASSOCIATION WITH
THE ATLANTIC MONTHLY PRESS

Published simultaneously in Canada
by Little, Brown & Company (Canada) Limited

PRINTED IN THE UNITED STATES OF AMERICA

Here
Lies
The
Body

Chapter 1

Everything we experienced, many long years ago, happened to us because my brother Mitch got a summer job mowing grass in a cemetery.

"In the cemetery?"

Mom sounded shocked. And naturally the first thing she did was scold us.

"Have you two been playing in the cemetery again? How many times have I told you —"

"We weren't *playing*, Mom." Mitch was scornful. After all, he was fifteen, and big for his age. Since I was only eleven I might still be accused of "playing," but not him.

"We don't play over there, we just walk around and look at things," he said. "We don't make any trouble, and nobody minds. Besides, it's interesting. There are some of the craziest old tombstones you ever saw. I'm going to write an article about them someday. But anyway, what happened was, we heard Mr. Zenger talking about being short of help for the summer, and he was wondering how they'd keep ahead of all that grass —"

"And you mean to tell me Ezekiel Zenger offered you a job?"

"Well, no. It was my idea."

"Mitch showed him how he could handle a lawn mower," I said with a hero-worshiper's voice, "and Mr. Zenger offered him twenty-five cents an hour!"

That was good money for a boy in those days. Mom could not help but be impressed.

"Well . . . We'll see what your father says."

Dad thought it was fine.

"Why not?" He grinned at us, knowing full well he was teasing Mom. "Mitch will be getting good wholesome exercise out in the open air in beautiful surroundings, and he'll be keeping company with the finest people in town. All the best old families are buried there."

"Not to mention some of the worst," retorted Mom.

"Well, you can't tell the worst from the best once they're six feet under, so they won't hurt him any. Twenty-five cents an hour! Why, son, you'll make a fortune. It just goes to show there's some advantage in living next to a rich cemetery."

But Mom was still having her doubts.

"Well, I don't know. Those old Zenger brothers give me the creeps."

Like all of us she knew them well by sight, because from our kitchen windows we could look over the wall into the cemetery. She often saw Ezekiel Zenger and his men working over there, mowing, trimming, planting flower beds, and — once — doing something she still remembered with a shudder.

"I'll never forget the way Ezekiel looked digging that grave," she said. "Singing and chuckling, as if he were having the time of his life. And then that old brother of his, Nathaniel . . . Every time I look out toward evening there he is, walking around over there in that black hat and that baggy black overcoat. Winter and summer I don't think I've ever seen him in anything else."

"Maybe his circulation is bad," said Dad. "Listen, it's a handy place for the old man to get his exercise, and I imagine he feels it's his privilege to make use of the grounds, since the land used to belong to his family. He has his private park right outside his door."

Nathaniel Zenger lived in the old family home next to the cemetery on the other side from us. The big ramshackle house, surrounded by century-old trees, stood on a point above the river. Ezekiel lived in a cottage on the same property, and the story was that the brothers lived apart because they hated each other.

"Well, all I can say is it depresses me every time I see him," said Mom in a gloomy voice. "That family has had a terrible history, from what I've heard. According to Eleanor Bradford . . ."

"And if anyone knows the gossip, ancient and modern, Eleanor does," said Dad, grinning again. Mrs. Bradford, president of the Historical Society, was our leading local historian, and Dad tended to make fun of people who spent their time poking around in the past. "But the Zengers can't be all bad. Don't forget, they *gave* the town the land for the cemetery."

"Bad conscience," Mom declared, "or an unhealthy interest in cemeteries. They've kept a death grip on it ever since."

Of course we all hooted at that.

"Death grip! That's pretty good," said Dad, but Mom went right on.

"Just the same, the Zengers have been connected with the cemetery in some capacity or other ever since they gave the land, and that's over two hundred years ago."

"And now they're down to one gravedigger. When he and his brother go that'll be the end of the Zengers, poor devils, so why pick on them?"

"I'm just not happy about my son working with a man who gives me the creeps."

"Well, he doesn't bother *me*, and I'm the one who will be cutting the grass," said Mitch.

In the end we talked her into it, but she still had a final word to say concerning the Zenger brothers.

"I'm just glad we live on this side of the cemetery and not theirs!"

Chapter 2

The cemetery was still called by its old name, Hemlock Hill Burial Ground. As we were to learn later, back before the turn of the century two members of the board of trustees decided the name was too old-fashioned. They wanted to change it to Hemlock Hill Cemetery.

The Zenger family was against it, but for a while it looked as if Colonel Duff and Dr. Roberts were going to get enough votes together among the other board members to have their way.

Then one night Dr. Roberts fell down the stairs in his home and broke his neck, and a few days later Colonel Duff died in a flash fire. After that nobody was left who wanted to make an issue of the name. So the colonel and the doctor were laid to rest in their family plots in Hemlock Hill Burial Ground, and it has kept that name to this day.

Mitch was hired to work afternoons, six days a week, for whatever amount of time Ezekiel Zenger decided he needed him each day. The first day he reported for work I was allowed to tag along. We climbed the stone wall at the back end of our property, dropped down into the cemetery, and headed for a small maintenance building where Ezekiel had told Mitch to show up at one o'clock.

Hemlock Hill Burial Ground was the oldest, biggest, and best cemetery in town, and also the richest. There was plenty of money available to keep everything in perfect order and provide for special touches, such as the annual spring tulip show and fall chrysanthemum show in the formal garden in front of the chapel.

Great elms and oaks, maples and chestnut trees towered at stately intervals, weeping willows drooped becomingly beside a pond, and smaller flowering trees touched up the landscape wherever another tree seemed called for. And underneath them spread a smooth carpet of green, lush and velvety, around the headstones and markers and tombs and mausoleums of marble, sandstone, granite, and slate, in shades running from white and gray to dull red, brown, and black. A mausoleum is a large tomb with room enough inside for several family coffins.

On a bright sunny June day it was quite a cheerful place, if you didn't mind some of the gloomier inscriptions. And Mitch, for one, didn't.

I had better explain about Mitch and the notebook he always carried in his hip pocket. At that time his big interest in life was writing — or maybe I should say playing with words, which is really the same thing. Mitch loved words, especially words that rhymed. He was already an editor on his high school newspaper, and besides that he was our family poet.

There used to be more of that sort of thing than there is now. It used to be that there was someone in every family — usually an elderly uncle, which was what made Mitch unusual — who wrote poems full of limping lines, gentle jokes, and painful puns for all social occasions. These would be read by the author with great personal satisfaction after dinner while the family was still gathered around the table, or if not there perhaps in front of the Christmas tree. This sort of thing:

> *Once more the Framidge family*
> *For Christmas gathered together be,*
> *With Grandpa and Grandma Framidge here*
> *To lend a bit of Yuletide cheer,*
> *And certainly let's not forget*
> *Auntie Jane and Auntie Bette*
> *Who provide against any mournful note*
> *A most effective auntie-dote ...*

Mitch's efforts were better than that. Elderly uncles tend to write lines that neither scan nor rhyme very well. Mitch tried harder. He was constantly scribbling in those days. It was natural and inevitable, then, that he should be fascinated with the inscriptions and some of the names that appeared on the various headstones and mausoleums and cenotaphs and other monuments in the cemetery.

"There's a name for you, Howie. Quackenbush!"

Mitch pointed to an old slate grave marker of the early eighteen hundreds and pulled up long enough to read the inscription on its tall, narrow face:

GONE AHEAD TO A LAND OF WONDER.

"Poor Quackenbush is six feet under," added Mitch, supplying a rhyme.

"You'd better watch that kind of stuff," I said. "He might not like it if he heard you."

"Who? Quackenbush?"

"No! Zenger!"

Mitch laughed and ran on ahead.

When we reached the maintenance shed Ezekiel Zenger was standing there waiting. He pulled out his big silver pocket watch, took a good look at it with squinty eyes, and seemed satisfied. Mitch was a couple of minutes ahead of time.

Ezekiel Zenger could have stood still and passed for a weathered statue on a graveyard monument himself, except that instead of looking like marble or granite he would have seemed to be fashioned out of the very earth around him. If ever there was an earthy man, it was he.

His big hands and his wrinkled face did not look

dirty, they simply looked earthy. He suggested the texture of earth. He smelled of earth. And he would certainly have left dusty fingerprints on anything he touched.

He was a large, powerful man with a big, broad face that made his bright blue eyes seem unexpectedly small. When he smiled the lines that crisscrossed his face were like the cracks that split the earth during a drought. There was no humor in his smile. When he smiled, you somehow wished he wouldn't.

But none of this bothered Mitch, who was thinking about twenty-five cents an hour and all that good reading material on the tombstones.

Ezekiel pointed to a lawn mower he had wheeled out of the shed. An old-fashioned reel mower, it was: lawn mowers did not depend on gasoline engines in those days, they depended on manpower, or in this case boypower.

"You can start by doing the Hawns," he told Mitch.

"The Hawns? Where's that?"

"The Hawns ain't *that*, they're *them*," snapped Ezekiel, giving us our first lesson in cemetery etiquette. "They're one of our oldest families, and they badly need doing."

"Oh. Well, where do I find them?"

Notice that Mitch said "them." He learned fast. Ezekiel turned and pointed.

"See the Duffs?"

It was not hard to pick out the Duffs. An imposing mausoleum with a dark winged angel poised on top of it stood on a slight rise about fifty yards away. Even though it was turned slightly away from us we could read DUFF graven into the marble above the iron-grilled door.

"I see them," said Mitch.

"Head for the Duffs, bear left to the Cranes, and you'll see the Hawns straight ahead down in the hollow," said Ezekiel. "Start there and cut all the grass that needs cutting in any direction. I'll be over later to see if you're making out well enough to hold down a job here. You're not just mowing some old lady's lawn now, you're working at Hemlock Hill, so keep that in mind."

"Yes, sir, I will."

"How's that?" snapped Ezekiel, and Mitch repeated what he had said in a louder voice.

"Oh. Well, see that you do."

Ezekiel turned his attention to me, looking down from what seemed an awesome height to an eleven-year-old who was still pretty much of a skinny shrimp.

"Who's this?"

"That's my brother."

They sounded as if they were discussing some insignificant piece of flotsam that had been cast up on a beach, but of course I didn't mind. I was only wondering why Ezekiel had bothered to take any notice of me at all. He had never bothered to notice me before.

"He wanted to come along and watch," Mitch went on to explain. "Is that all right?"

"He what? Speak up, boy, don't mumble!" said Ezekiel, and Mitch repeated what he had said, though it seemed to me he had spoken up pretty well in the first place. It began to be apparent that Ezekiel was a mite deaf.

"Hmm." Ezekiel looked me over. "The Devil finds work for idle hands, so mebbe I better beat him to it."

He turned and disappeared into the shed. Before we could do more than stare at each other he was back with a pair of flat-bladed clippers.

"Grass has to be trimmed around every headstone and marker and everything else," he said, snapping the clippers' blades together. I can still hear the hard slide of metal against metal. "If it's carefully done, well and carefully done, he might as well be making himself ten cents an hour as standing around with his hands in his pockets."

My head swam, my pulses raced. It took all I could do to remain as noncommittal as a native New Englander is supposed to remain in the face of pleasure. *I* was being offered a job too!

I held out my hand for the clippers and said, "Sure!" And I am very much afraid that single word betrayed some of my excitement.

Chapter 3

Mitch flipped the lawn mower over so that its blades were up out of the way and started wheeling it toward the Duffs with me trotting along beside him. I was doing my best to look like the kind of workman you could depend on.

I could hardly wait to talk about my good fortune. As soon as we had put a couple of family plots between us and Ezekiel, and a quick glance over my shoulder told me he had gone back into the shed anyway, I burst out.

"How do you like that? Did you ever hear of anything so lucky?"

I didn't have to explain what I meant. The point was, when we did the lawn at home we had the same two jobs. Mitch pushed the lawn mower and I did the trimming around the flower beds and bushes and along the sides of the front walk and the driveway. Those hours spent on my hands and knees had never thrilled me at the time, but now they were going to pay off.

"You're lucky, all right," said Mitch gruffly. Naturally it didn't altogether please him to have his kid brother steal some of his glory. It took him a minute to get used to the idea. "Well, if you're going to work with me you're going to *work*, and not fool around the way you do sometimes at home."

"Don't you worry!"

We walked up the slope to the Duff mausoleum. Mitch tilted his head back for a long look and muttered,

"Gloomy Gus."

"What?"

"That angel."

The big winged figure was made of bronze, and even at midday it was dark against the bright sky. In spite of the fact that I was especially happy at the moment, it dampened my spirits just to look up at that hard and merciless face. I had never seen a less gentle-looking angel. Perched on one foot on the top point of the mausoleum, the figure strained forward with one arm flung out straight ahead and a finger pointing as if he were cursing someone rather than blessing him.

The gesture was so compelling I found myself turning to look where the angel was pointing. Off to the left of the maintenance shed was a large plot set apart by low, square granite posts with green chain looping from one to the next, but at that distance I could not read any names on the stones, which looked very old.

"What's he pointing at?" I wondered aloud, and Mitch answered so promptly I realized he must have been affected the same way I was.

"Must be those folks over there," he said. "I hope it doesn't make them nervous. Sometime we'll have to go over and find out who they are."

Mitch stopped in front of the Duff mausoleum, mumbled, "Bear left to the Cranes," and made a great show of shading his eyes and peering off to the left. It wasn't necessary, because a marker in the form of a big natural boulder with CRANE carved into it was in plain sight about fifty yards away. Wheeling the lawn mower expertly between mounds and around tombstones, Mitch set his course for the Cranes.

When we reached the boulder we found the land sloped off just beyond the Crane family plot, and there below us in a hollow was a big, neatly marked-off plot with a large gray granite cenotaph in the center of it. A cenotaph is a tall shaft, squared off and slightly tapering, shaped like the Washington Monument. The name on the base of the cenotaph was HAWN.

"Hawn," said Mitch thoughtfully. "Hawn."

Anyone else might have thought he was trying to recall where he had heard the name before, but I knew better. He was probably thinking about what would rhyme with it.

"Okay, let's go down and get started," said Mitch. "I want to make a good showing."

A minute later we were a picture of industry, with the lawn-mower blades whirring and the clippers zinging. Ezekiel had been right, the Hawns badly needed doing. The grass was high everywhere, and thick and straggly around the tombstones. We were both going to earn our money.

For quite a while we worked without pause, and not a soul came near us, Ezekiel or anybody else. Nobody was even in sight. Presently Mitch began to chuckle.

"What's the matter?"

He gave me a kind of glance I had learned to recognize, which didn't make it any easier to live with.

"Don't bother me. Tell you later."

He was composing. If you have ever been around anyone like Mitch you know how exasperating it was for me. I knew he was thinking up something, prob-ably something funny, but I was shut out of his thoughts and had to wait around, with my curiosity aroused, until he was good and ready to spring his latest effort on me.

After a while he started chuckling again and grin-ning to himself. It was more annoying than the first time.

"What is it now?" I snapped at him.

He stopped and pulled out his notebook and pencil.

"I'd better write them down before I forget them," he muttered. He flipped open his grubby notebook and started to scribble. I waited impatiently, but no longer as irritably. Once he wrote things down he usually read them to me. And true to form, when he finished he faced me with a grin, that special self-satisfied smirk of the creative artist.

"Listen to this," he ordered, and read his first production in a deep, doleful voice, like a voice from a tomb:

> *Here lies the body of Harvey Hawn;*
> *Waylaid at midnight, slaughtered at dawn.*

I laughed, forgiving him now. Then I glanced around at the tombstones.

"Where's Harvey?"

Mitch gave me a poet's withering look.

"I made up 'Harvey,' you dummy," he said. "That's what's called alliteration, using the same first letter as the next word. Listen to this one."

Again he read in the same dismal voice:

> *Here lies the body of Carolyn Crane;*
> *Somebody pushed her in front of a train.*

This time I sat back on my heels and snickered approvingly. To hear people talk today you would think black humor, or sick humor, or gallows humor — there are lots of names for it — is a modern invention, but it's always been around, and kids have always loved it. The grislier the better. We grinned at each other like two fiends.

The creative urge had thoroughly seized Mitch.

"You know what?" he said, as he stuck his notebook and pencil back in his pocket. "I'm going to do a whole alphabet, and then sometime after we've quit working here I'll read them to Mom and Dad. Can't you just hear her?"

Our howls of laughter showed that we could both hear her loud and clear. She would try — unsuccessfully — not to laugh. She would say, "Mitchell Bell, that's terrible! I don't want to hear any more!" But Mitch would go right on, and she would keep listening. And Dad, of course, would enjoy it all thoroughly.

Collecting himself and remembering where we were, Mitch took a quick guilty look around and said, "We'd better get back to work," and we both went at it again with renewed industry. I clipped away, having to use both hands when the grass was thick and tough, and beginning to realize I might end up with some blisters before I was through. And thinking, oh, well, before long they would be calluses. Presently I was clipping around a small round-topped stone that said in worn letters:

Our beloved infant son
TIMOTHY
Aged 3 years 2 months
April 3, 1834

Back in those days, we learned, lots of children did not live very long. The tombstones of people who had lived into their eighties never bothered us, but those little stones were depressing.

We put in another good spell of work and then Mitch began to chuckle again. This time I didn't say anything. I just waited till he stopped and pulled out his pencil and notebook, and watched him scribble. Then I said,

"Let's hear it."

From the way he looked I knew he had come up with one he specially liked. He read it to me:

Here lies the body of Dudley Duff;
Lightning struck twice, though once was enough.

I thought that was pretty funny, and so did he, and by then we felt so alone in the world — except for the Hawns — that we gave free expression to our mirth, as the saying goes. But Mitch had hardly put away his notebook and pencil and started pushing the lawn mower again before Ezekiel suddenly appeared on the ridge up by the Cranes and came stumping down toward us.

He didn't look pleased. After each of us had noted his approach with quick and furtive glances the whirring and zinging suggested new levels of industry.

He came toward us like some Old Testament figure, monumental and menacing, but he spoke like a New Englander — not that some of them are not straight out of the Old Testament.

"Seems to me I heard a lot of guffawing going on down here," he declared with a heavy frown.

He might be deaf, but obviously we had registered even on his ears. We stared around at him with scared eyes, and neither of us spoke. We could feel our jobs hanging in the balance.

And then Mitch managed to say exactly the right thing without knowing it.

"I'm sorry, Mr. Zenger. I guess we were just nervous."

"*Nervous?*"

Ezekiel spoke the word as if it were ridiculous, and yet we could sense that he had accepted Mitch's answer. He seemed to relax, and he smiled slightly, just for an instant. We wished he hadn't. Even though we knew we were about to be forgiven, we could have done without that smile.

"Ain't nothing to be nervous about," he declared, still putting up a front of being severe. "If I thought you were going to act fidgety I'd send you packing. However . . . You'll get used to it. Just remember that everyone in this cemetery is dead, and they're going to stay dead."

"Yes, sir!"

He prowled around with heavy steps, looking over our work. His leather boots with the cuffs of corduroy trousers stuck into them were the color of the dust imbedded in them. After a while he nodded, a grudging New England nod.

"Well, you've made a start. We'll see. We'll see. But I want the Hawns to look up to snuff when you're finished, you hear me? If they're not, you won't be coming back tomorrow."

"Yes, sir!"

"I'll be back," he promised grimly. "Get to work."

"Yes, sir!"

By the time we finished, the Hawns were up to snuff.

And we were glad Ezekiel Zenger had not shown up in time to hear about how Harvey Hawn was slaughtered at dawn.

Chapter 4

You can imagine how the news was received at home that both of us had landed a job in the cemetery.

Dad thought it was fine. Mom looked as if she had lost her sons.

"It's bad enough to have Mitch over there, but Howie, at his age . . ."

"But if he's going to hang around with Mitch he might as well be getting some pocket money out of it."

"Ezekiel said the Devil finds work for idle hands so maybe he'd better beat him to it," quoted Mitch.

"He's right, son. Well, anyway, how did it go today?"

"We did the Hawns."

"And they badly needed doing," I said, adding a quote myself.

"They what?"

"That's what Ezekiel said."

"And they sure did. The grass was practically up to our waists," said Mitch, exaggerating a little, as poets will. "But we did a good job, and we can come back tomorrow."

He laughed.

"The way Ezekiel gives directions is funny! Go over to the Duffs, bear left to the Cranes, and the Hawns are straight ahead down in the hollow."

"The Duffs, eh?" said Dad. "That reminds me, I saw George Bird today and I was telling him about Mitch's new job. George is on the cemetery's board of trustees. Anyway, George told me an interesting yarn about why it's still called Hemlock Hill Burial Ground . . ."

It was then we heard the story about how Colonel Duff and Dr. Roberts had tried to change the name. When we heard "Duff" mentioned Mitch and I exchanged a glance but didn't interrupt the story. Neither did Mom until Dad came to the part about how both men had died.

"I told you those Zengers were a bad lot," she said.

"Well, of course it did seem odd, the two of them dying so close together, but I don't see how you can blame the Zengers. Anyway, it all happened nearly fifty years ago."

"If you want to see something creepy, you ought to see the statue on top of the Duffs' mausoleum," said Mitch.

"George mentioned that," Dad surprised us by

24

replying. "Seems that after the colonel died his son had that statue put up there, and George says it caused a lot of talk at the time, though he couldn't recall why."

That sent another glance shooting between Mitch and me, but with Mom there we both decided not to comment. That night, though, I dreamt about that dark figure with its hard face and its pointing finger, and I woke up scared.

The next afternoon we did the Griffs.

They didn't need doing as badly as the Hawns had, but nevertheless they required a good deal of attention. They were easier on my hands than the Hawns had been, which was just as well, since I had a blister or two from my first day's work which I had been careful not to let Mom see.

"Joe Palermo's tending to a flower bed over near the sheds," Ezekiel told us when we reported for work. "Follow that road till you see Joe, and he'll tell you where the Griffs are."

With Mitch pushing his lawn mower and me carrying my clippers, we set out along one of the gravel roads that wound through the grounds.

Mitch had not forgotten his notebook. As we walked along his eyes were taking in every hand-carved name we passed.

"Watch for Qs and Xs," he said. "Those will be the tough ones to find."

"How about Quackenbush?"

"Quackenbush! For Pete's sake, what can you rhyme with Quackenbush? I've got to find another Q."

We hadn't gone far before he stopped short and pointed to a headstone.

"There's a dandy *V!* I've got a *great* rhyme for that one! Here, push this thing for me so we can keep going while I write." We were not out of Ezekiel's sight yet, if he happened to be looking, so it would have been foolhardy to stop and scribble on company time.

I stuck my clippers through my belt and took charge of the lawn mower. Before I had even figured out how the name might be pronounced, our family poet had finished and was reading me his version of it:

Here lies the body of Vladimir Varsenik;
It must have been something he ate, like arsenic.

Before we came to where Joe Palermo was working Mitch had knocked off *J* and *A*, too, as follows:

Here lies the body of Jasmine Jones;
On Halloween nights you can hear her groans.

Here lies the body of Arty Alfredo;
Nobody warned him about the tornado.

We didn't see any sheds anywhere, but pretty soon

we saw a workman down on his knees beside a flower bed, and some tombstones nearby explained the confusion.

"Oh. The *Shedds*," said Mitch. "We might have known."

The day was bright and sunny, and so was the face of the man who glanced around at us when he heard us coming.

"Hi," said Mitch. "Are you Mr. Palermo?"

"That's right. I'm Joe," he said, and we knew that was what we could call him.

"I'm Mitch, and he's Howie. Mr. Zenger said you'd tell us where the Griffs are."

"Sure." Joe sat back on his plump haunches and pointed. "Over there."

He turned to us again. The smile on his round face made us feel good.

"You did a good job on the Hawns, boys. I saw."

"Mr. Zenger said it would do," Mitch told him, and Joe laughed.

"Zeke ain't gonna kiss you on both cheeks no matter how good you are, but if he says it'll do it's okay. Where you live?"

"Just the other side of the wall on Prentiss Street."

"You're lucky. I gotta drive two, three miles from my house. Okay, you go do the Griffs."

We thanked him and left him busy with the bed of zinnias he was weeding. We detoured around some visitors who were putting flowers on a grave and found the Griffs. They had a cenotaph in the middle of their family plot, too. It looked a lot like the Hawns', except that it was sort of blue-gray instead of gray. I noticed their dates didn't go back as far as the Hawns', either.

We went to work mowing and trimming. I started out by clipping the grass around the base of the cenotaph. After a while a big fly started buzzing around, bothering me. I took a swing at him and my clippers hit the side of the cenotaph.

Instead of just gritting against the metal the way granite would, it gave off a booming sound. I rocked back away from it, amazed.

"Hey, Mitch, did you hear that?"

I tapped it again. Another strange boom.

"This thing sounds hollow!"

Mitch examined the tall shaft closely and tapped it himself.

"My gosh, it is! This thing isn't stone at all, it's made of cast iron or something. Anyway, it's metal. I guess that was one way to put on a show and still save money."

You run across lots of odd things in a cemetery.

We got busy again. And of course all the time I was wondering how soon the notebook would come out. Last night Mitch had written the alphabet on the first page so he could cross off letters as he did them.

After a while there came the familiar chuckle and he stopped to scribble. When he had finished we both glanced around, because we were pretty much out in the open where the Griffs were.

"Okay, let's hear it," I said, and Mitch read:

Here lies the body of Septimus Shedd —
Minus a finger or two and a head.

We kept our snickering low-key this time, having learned our lesson, but I was hungering for more and said, "How about the Griffs?"

"All taken care of," said Mitch, and looked as if he were going to read some more, but then all of a sudden the notebook and pencil went flying back into his pocket as he glanced past me.

"Get busy," he muttered. "Here comes Zeke."

Fortunately Ezekiel stopped to talk to Joe for a minute, so we were able to produce plenty of industrious sounds before he came on over to where we were. His small bright blue eyes darted around professionally, missing nothing, and he nodded as though satisfied.

"You can work a little longer today," he said. "When you finish here go over and do the Quigleys."

"The Quigleys?" cried Mitch before he could stop himself, and got a sharp look from Ezekiel.

"That's what I said. What's the matter?"

"Oh, uh, I know somebody named Quigley," said Mitch, floundering a little. He couldn't very well explain he was excited because the name began with Q. "Where are they?"

Ezekiel pointed.

"Head for the Manettos and keep going. And be careful around them old slate headstones over that-away, they're a mite shaky. Need resetting, most of 'em, when I can get to it. You seen Barney Ryan anywheres?"

"Who's he?"

"Tall skinny feller. He's supposed to be doing the Hathaways, but he ain't there. If he's loafing again it'll go hard with him."

"Well, he hasn't been around here, has he, Howie?"

Ezekiel gave us a short nod and stumped off again, growling to himself. We both felt we wouldn't care to get caught loafing by Ezekiel Zenger. Mitch got the lawn mower going briskly again, but while he worked he was muttering under his breath.

"Quigley," he was saying, "Quigley..."

As soon as Ezekiel was a fair distance away I said in a low voice,

"Okay, now about the Griffs?"

"Later!" snapped Mitch, keeping the lawn mower going. "He may not hear too well but there's nothing wrong with his eyesight."

"But can't you just remember it without having to get out your notebook?"

"Well..."

The poet was tempted. He stopped and crouched down beside the lawn mower, pretending to be clearing the blades of bunches of grass, and recited:

Here lies the body of Gwendolyn Griff,
Last seen alive near the edge of a cliff.

"It'll do," I said, mimicking Ezekiel. "Cross off G. Hey, how about Hathaway?" I went on, remembering the family Barney Ryan was supposed to be doing. "There's a dandy name!"

But Mitch frowned and shook his head.

"You can really pick 'em! Hathaway's as bad as Quackenbush. Anyway, I've already got Hawn for H."

We went back to work, but I kept thinking about my latest suggestion, and all of a sudden I had a flash of inspiration. I stopped clipping and swung around to Mitch.

"How's this?" I cried, and recited eagerly:

Here lies the body of Herbie Hathaway;
He went for a walk in the dark on the edge of a
cliff but someone cut the path away!

Mitch stopped and stared at me, wincing and snickering at the same time.

"Terrible! You stole the cliff from the Griffs, and your second line's about a block too long," he said. But he was still snickering. "I've got to admit one thing, though — your rhyme's a pip!"

I think that was the first inkling I ever had that maybe someday I too might want to write.

Chapter 5

Our New England weather is always changeable in June, but I don't think it was ever more so than that year. By the time we were nearly finished doing the Quigleys the fine weather had gone, the sky had clouded up, and it looked as if it might pour any minute.

On our way over the Manettos had gotten theirs:

> *Here lies the body of Marty Manetto,*
> *Stabbed in the back with a poisoned stiletto.*

And before long Mitch had taken care of the Quigleys as well:

> *Here lies the body of Quentin Quigley,*
> *Done to death by something wriggly.*

He was feeling very good about that.

"Hey, boys!"

It was Joe calling to us from quite a distance, clear over by the Cranes.

"Zeke wants you to quit," he called. "Bring your tools back to the shed."

We wasted no time knocking off work and high-tailing it for cover. Under ominous clouds that made dark caves of the shadows under the big trees the cemetery had turned into a different place, dreary and oppressive, with a somber atmosphere that made both of us uneasy, even though we put on a great show of ignoring it by chattering in a smart-alecky vein along the way. We made little jokes about how gloomy it was, but we tended to speak in low voices, as though someone might be listening, and not necessarily Ezekiel Zenger.

The Duff mausoleum loomed up ahead of us with that dark figure on top of it and I was just as glad it was facing away from us. And yet when we had passed it I could not resist glancing back over my shoulder. The angel was a black silhouette against a gray sky.

Nobody was in sight when we reached the shed. Everything was still, the way it is before a storm. Not a leaf rustled, not a blade of grass stirred. Mitch's voice was a murmur, as if he were afraid to break the silence.

"Let's put our stuff away and get going!"

Inside the shadowy shed smelled of loam, of mold

and mildew. What had been pleasantly earthy when the sun was shining was something else now. We got out again as fast as we could.

When we came outside it was I who noticed the crouching figure in the large family burial ground off to the left of the maintenance shed. Maybe that was because by then my eyes were even busier than Mitch's, darting around in every direction. At any rate, I saw it, and grabbed my brother's arm, and breathed a single word.

"Look."

The massive figure was unmistakable, even through the trees and at a distance of a hundred feet. It was Ezekiel, and he was down in front of a flat slate headstone, scrubbing away at it. We had not made much noise, in spite of the lawn mower, and obviously he had not heard us.

"What's he doing?" I whispered, and Mitch hissed, "How should I know?" and nudged me fiercely to be quiet.

An instant later we both pressed ourselves against the side of the shed under the low eaves and held our breath. Because suddenly another familiar figure appeared. It was one we had often seen and laughed at from our kitchen windows, but now, away from the security of our own home, neither of us had the slightest impulse to laugh.

His profile loomed skull-like under the broad-brimmed black hat. Ancient, mottled parchment rather than living skin stretched across it. His bulging forehead hung over dark eyes burning deep in the shadows of their sockets. His broad mouth, when its thin lips stretched in a grin, bared a crooked line of yellowed teeth. We had never seen him this close before, and anything that had seemed comical at a distance no longer offered us that comfort. I think if he had glanced our way and noticed us I would have screamed.

Ezekiel looked up at the cadaverous figure in the black hat and the baggy black overcoat. Then he came to his feet. He did not spring to his feet — earthen mountains do not spring — but he came quickly to his feet.

"You did this, you Devil's whelp, and I'll not have it!" he snarled.

Nathaniel made a sound deep in his throat. Maybe it was supposed to be laughter.

"Why, brother, what is it now?"

"You know what it is, and if it happens again I swear I'll put the police on you and your — your —"

Again we heard that hollow, choking sound, whatever it was intended to be.

"The police!" said Nathaniel, and his voice dripped with contempt. "You won't call the police."

"I will!"

"Then do so. Do so, for all the good —"

I am sure both Mitch and I lost a few years of life at that moment. Because the air was split with a white flash of lightning that made both Zenger brothers stand out lividly like figures in a photographic nega-

35

tive. Then thunder boomed in our ears so quickly that we knew a bolt had struck close by. All I remember is being plastered against the side of the shed as if it were my last hope, and seeing Mitch's face briefly in that flash of lightning, a face as terrifyingly pale as my own must have been.

It was a moment before we could find the courage to move a muscle, let alone do anything such as taking another look at the scene we had been watching.

When we did look, both brothers were gone. They were gone, and Mitch had a kid brother who was terrified.

"I'm going home!"

Poets are a strange breed. They seem able to stand anything except unsatisfied curiosity, they will dare anything rather than miss the answer to a question they want answered.

"They're gone," he said. "Come on, I want to see that stone."

And he began to sprint toward the burial ground where we had seen the brothers.

It was a long way home across the length of Hemlock Hill Burial Ground, and a short way to catch up with Mitch. It is not hard to guess which direction I ran, in spite of my terror.

Mitch had made a dead set on the proper headstone. By that I mean he had made careful note of which one in the forest of headstones in that family plot it was that Ezekiel Zenger had been crouched down in front of, scrubbing away at. When we

reached it I don't suppose either of us was surprised by the family name we saw on the flaking seventeenth-century headstone.

The first name was MICAH. The family name was ZENGER.

We were in the Zenger family burial ground.

Mitch was not thinking about that, however. He was down on his knees in front of the stone, while thunder rolled again, staring at the face of it and a blur above the name and the date "d. 1698."

In spite of all the scrubbing Ezekiel had done, the threat of rain had stopped him short. We could still see the faint outline, in dark red, of a symbol which at that moment meant nothing to us.

The bottom part of it looked like part of a cross, like a T with the bottom line spread into a triangle. On top of this T was a hollow circle, and on top of that a pair of points like horns.

"What is it, Mitch?"

He seemed to be trembling.

"I don't know," he said, "but it's something evil. I can feel it."

His words frightened me badly — because I could feel it too.

Lightning flashed again and thunder crashed, though not as close this time. Mitch sprang to his feet.

"Let's go! And stay away from lone trees!" he ordered, mindful of what he had heard about the targets lightning bolts picked.

38

We turned to go when the same sight stopped us both in our tracks. Lighted by a crooked fork of lightning in the distance behind it, the dark figure on the Duff mausoleum dominated the stormy sky. And that rigid finger was pointed straight our way. Straight at the Zenger burial ground.

Chapter 6

Too late, we ran for home. While lightning flashed and thunder rolled, we ran past the Duffs and that terrible angel, past the Manettos and the Shedds, the Griffs and the Quigleys. I threw a glance back at the place we had fled from. It looked like one of those grim steel engravings that hung in funereal frames in our grandfather's old-fashioned parlor, all grays and blacks, gray skies and black shadows. And then one great crack of thunder seemed to split the skies open.

First a few big drops spattered in the dust of the road ahead of us. Then the rain came down like a curtain. The Duff mausoleum, the statue, the Zenger graveyard — all disappeared, blotted out. I gasped at the unexpected icy chill of the downpour. It dropped our pace to a discouraged trot.

"No use running," Mitch panted. "We can't get any wetter than we already are."

40

From then on we plodded home, the grass squelching soggily under our soaked sneakers. We were both breathing too hard to do any talking. That could wait till we were safe inside.

When at last we had scrambled over the wet, slippery stones of the wall and crossed our back lawn, we were glad to find ourselves alone in the house. We were in no mood to answer questions with half-truths, knowing that any mention of what had really gone on in the cemetery would put Mom in an uproar.

We took off our clothes in the kitchen, wrung them out in the sink, and hung them on a line on the back porch. Before he hung up his pants Mitch dug his notebook out of a back pocket. He had buttoned a flap over it and it had come through pretty well, only a little damp around the edges.

We dried off in the bathroom and put on fresh clothes. Mitch pulled his on in a hurry, obviously having something on his mind he wanted to get to. A moment later he sat down at his desk and grabbed a pencil and a sheet of paper.

"I want to draw that thing we saw before I forget it," he muttered.

"Don't worry, I'll *never* forget it!" A shiver made my teeth chatter. "That rain was regular ice water!" I added quickly, to account for my shaking.

Mitch was paying no attention to me, however. He was busy drawing. I watched over his shoulder and made a few comments — "No, the horns were longer," and "That's right, like a triangle."

'After a few erasures and corrections Mitch had a drawing that satisfied both of us. It looked like this:

We stared at it uneasily for a while. Finally I said, "The way they were acting, Nathaniel must have painted that on the headstone."

"Either Nathaniel or someone he knows. Someone who was there with him. You heard what Zeke said."

Even then Mitch had a good ear for dialogue and could recall it word for word when he was interested enough to listen closely. He did so now.

"Zeke said, 'You know what it is, and if it happens again I swear I'll put the police on you and your — your —' "

"I know, I heard him. I wish he had finished what he was going to say."

"So do I. One more word, and we'd know a lot more."

Mitch stared at his drawing. I sat on the edge of my bed and shivered again.

"What do *you* think it means, Mitch?"

He shrugged irritably. As always, it annoyed him to be stumped.

"How should I know? All I know is it doesn't look like any Sunday school symbol."

"That's for sure. It looks . . ."

As I hesitated, trying to think of the right word, Mitch's head came up and his eyes darted at me intently.

"Evil?" said Mitch, and when you think about it that was strange, because that was the second time he had spoken the word to describe the symbol, and "evil" was not a natural word for him to use. Bad, lousy, rotten, but not evil. And yet at that moment it did not sound odd. It sounded inevitable.

Of course, we had both used the word many times in one way: "Deliver us from evil . . ."

Evil . . .

"That's about it," I admitted.

"Of course, seeing it where we did and the way we did was enough to make anything give us the creeps. Those two old guys . . ."

I asked a question then that had been bothering me as much as the mystery of the symbol.

"Mitch, where did they go?"

He frowned at me and tried to treat the question as if it were silly.

"Well, where do you think? They took off to get out of the rain!"

"Did you see them go?"

"No!"

"Neither did I."

Mitch fidgeted.

"Well, so what? I wasn't looking. That first clap of thunder nearly scared the life out of me, I don't mind telling you. I thought the end of the world had come!"

"So did I!"

"I guess watching those two had us nerved up already, and that big bang really put the finishing touches on it. By the time I looked again they were gone."

"Same here."

"They got moving in a hurry, I guess. What did you think, Howie? Did you think they'd taken off on a couple of broomsticks?"

"Zeke?"

Mitch's challenging expression went blank, and then we both started whooping with laughter. The thought of Ezekiel on a broomstick was too much.

"It would take some hunk of broomstick to get *him* off the ground!" Mitch choked. Ezekiel was someone meant to keep his feet planted solidly on the earth. Anything else was unthinkable.

It took us a while to recover, and by then we felt better. But even so, when he had stopped laughing Mitch began to look thoughtful again.

"But Nathaniel, now . . ." he said, and we looked at each other, and I became thoughtful too. Skinny, cadaverous, bony, with his baggy overcoat flapping around him . . .

"He could make it," I agreed.

We thought about that for a spell, while the rain beat against the windows Mom had carefully closed before going out. Finally a notion made me grin.

"Tell you what, Mitch — tomorrow you can *ask* Zeke where they went."

"Remind me to do that. Boy! I can see myself now!"

He picked up his pencil and twiddled it between his fingers, drumming on the desk with the eraser end as he studied the drawing again.

"But I'll tell you what I *am* going to do tomorrow. First thing in the morning I'm going to the library and see if I can find something that will tell us what this thing *does* mean."

It was still raining so hard we didn't hear the car come up the driveway. I glanced out the window in time to see Mom running toward the house under an umbrella.

"Here comes Mom."

"Yeah. Don't say a word about —"

"Course not!"

We headed for the kitchen.

"We got caught in the rain, Mom," Mitch called to her.

"I sort of figured you might have from the looks of the line out here," she replied from the porch. "Did you two dry off properly?"

Fortunately she did not ask any questions that were not routine and easy to answer. Mitch slipped away after a minute or two, and I heard his desk drawer open and close. He had put the drawing out of sight.

Chapter 7

Instead of clearing up the way they usually do the day after a summer thunderstorm, the skies next morning were still weighted down with heavy gray clouds.

It was the kind of morning when New Englanders assure each other, "It'll burn off by ten o'clock," meaning the sun will break through by then and scatter the clouds. When we walked to the library, however, the gloom was still with us. I was not looking forward to reporting for work that afternoon.

For one thing, the thought of facing Ezekiel again scared me.

On the other hand, something even more disturbing was bothering me: the thought of *not* seeing Ezekiel again. Of finding he was not there anymore.

It made me mad to catch myself thinking such a

crazy thing. I didn't know then that irrational thoughts will not always go away simply because you tell yourself they are irrational. And of course I didn't say a word about all this to Mitch, except in an indirect way:

"We sure will earn our dough today," I grumbled.

"Well, if it stays like this it'll be too wet to work anyway."

I tried not to look too hopeful.

Our local branch library was only a few blocks from our house. We both read a lot, so we went there often. We said good morning to a couple of the librarians and Mitch made straight for the main catalog.

But then he hesitated. Typically, he had been so confident he would be able to find what he wanted in short order that he had not yet stopped to pin down exactly what subject he would look under.

"Hmm," he said, and tried to act as if he were merely hesitating between a couple of choices he had in mind. Also typically, I had been depending on him, and therefore had not given the matter serious thought. Now I did, but without immediate success.

"What are you going to look under?" I asked.

"A flat stone," said Mitch, playing for time by cracking a joke. "Let me see, now . . ."

"Why not ask a librarian?"

"Oh, sure — and then have them start asking *us* questions!"

He was right, of course. How could we explain what we were interested in?

A category occurred to me, but it was almost embarrassing to mention it, because it made me sound like some kid who still believed in Halloween. Nevertheless, I spit it out.

"How about witchcraft?"

Mitch gave me a flustered glance that made it plain the same thing had occurred to him. But of course he pretended otherwise.

"*Witchcraft?*" he said, bringing the scorn of his full fifteen years into his tone of voice. "What's the matter, you still got broomsticks on your mind?"

Before I could think of a suitable comeback, another library patron came bustling in with her usual purposeful stride, like a hen who has her eyes on a scattering of kernels she intends to peck up without another moment's delay.

She was a short, plump lady with tightly curled reddish hair. The jowls of her round cheeks trembled like wattles when jarred by her quick steps, but the mouth between them was small and firm. Her brown eyes glittered brightly behind small, rimless glasses. She was carrying the large, floppy, tapestry-covered bag, almost a satchel, that was always with her on her frequent trips to the library.

"Good morning, boys!"

"Good morning, Mrs. Bradford."

She sang a good-morning in her odd, clucking voice to the librarians, all old acquaintances of hers, and marched straight for a small room in one corner of the library. Over the door was a brass plaque: The Silas P. Bradford New England Historical Collection.

The collection of local history books had been left to the library by her late husband's grandfather, and she made more use of it than anyone else in town.

Mrs. Bradford saved the day for Mitch. The minute he saw her his eyes lighted up. When she had gone by he turned to me and jerked his head her way.

"Why didn't I think of her?"

"What do you mean?"

"Well, if anyone can tell us —"

"I thought you didn't want to talk to anyone about it."

"Not the librarians, I meant. They'd ask too many questions."

"So will she."

"I know, but . . . well, I've got a hunch it will be worth it." He glanced at me and explained. "I remember a piece she wrote once in the Sunday paper. It was about this kind of stuff."

As president of the local Historical Society, which she loved to refer to as the "Hysterical Society," Mrs. Bradford wrote a column about local history that appeared once a month in our Sunday paper.

By the time we reached the Bradford Room she was already settled at a small table in front of the window, digging things out of her bag, which she always called her "office." Out of it came notebooks, a scratch pad, pencils with needle-sharp points, and a couple of pamphlets, as she readied herself to go to work.

When we craned our necks through the doorway, hesitating to walk right in, she glanced up over the top of her glasses.

"Well, boys?" Immediately her eyes lit up with a fanatic's zeal, with the hope that we were about to show interest in some aspect of local history. "Are you looking for something? Can I help you?"

Close up, Mitch's self-assurance had deserted him. He shuffled his feet and said, "Well . . . It's just something we were wondering about."

"Good. A little curiosity never hurt anybody, no matter what they say about cats. What sort of thing?"

"Why, uh, a sort of sign, or symbol, whatever you call it. I thought maybe you would know what it stands for."

"I see. What does it look like?"

Mitch pulled the drawing out of his pocket.

"I had to draw this from memory, so it's not very good, but. . ."

He held it out to her. Smiling helpfully, Mrs. Bradford accepted it with one hand while she adjusted her glasses with the other, pushing them up on her snub nose. Then she looked at the drawing.

Her reaction made us start. Her small mouth pursed together as she caught her breath sharply, and the smile was gone. Her eyes went wide as she stared up at Mitch.

"Where did you see this?"

She almost hissed the question in a low voice, and then, thinking better of it, held a finger to her lips, leaving Mitch with his mouth open before he could reply. Her glance flicked past us toward the door, and her meaning was clear. Whatever the symbol stood for, she did not want to discuss it there, where others might overhear.

She handed the drawing back to Mitch. When she spoke her voice was calm again, but she still kept it to a murmur.

"This is very interesting, and I'd like to talk to you about it, but I have to do some work right now, so could you come over to my house in about an hour?"

"Sure."

"I'll be home by then and we'll have a talk."

Their eyes met like conspirators', and the excitement we felt fed on the aroused light that still glinted in hers. We turned and left, hurrying out of the library so abruptly we almost bumped into old Mr. Carpenter, coming in to read the local paper as he did every morning.

We rushed down the street, going nowhere, savoring the drama we had just been part of, glancing around to make sure no one was near before we finally began to talk about it.

The atmosphere of that gray morning was still the same, but now it took on new dimensions, new depths. Humdrum realities gave way to a sense of something unseen, something just around the corner somewhere, a shadowy force we did not understand.

"I had the right hunch *that* time," muttered Mitch. "She knows what it is, all right, and it gave her a jolt."

"She gave *me* a jolt! I wish she'd said she would come home right away. An hour, for Pete's sake! What are we going to do for an hour?"

Under the circumstances an hour seemed an eternity. But Mitch thought of a way to pass the time. A new kind of excitement added itself to what was already stirring him.

"I'll tell you what we'll do. We'll walk over to the cemetery and see if we can find Zeke!"

"What? Listen, if he ever got the idea we were spying on him —"

But Mitch was having one of his attacks of cleverness. He chuckled.

"Don't worry, it won't look that way, because I'll tell him we just wanted to find out if we're to come to work this afternoon."

Not bad. It was the sort of idea you had to go along with, even when the thought of what you might find — or not find— was enough to give you goose-flesh.

From where we were the main entrance was the closest way into Hemlock Hill Burial Ground. In less than ten minutes we were walking past the lavish layout of flower beds that lined the approach to the tall wrought-iron gates. Opened wide for the day, a pair of them flanked both entrances on either side of a huge boulder that bore the cemetery's name in plain, unobtrusive lettering.

It may be that Mitch felt no more certain than I that we would find Ezekiel there at all. As we walked through the grounds toward the maintenance shed, not a soul was in evidence. The chapel, vaguely medieval in gray granite, was a silent sentinel in a dreary landscape. It sounds facetious to describe a cemetery as lifeless, but at that moment the only sign of life was ourselves.

The trees, their leaves still heavy with a slick of wet, were motionless. Flowers, beaten down by the rain, drooped soddenly over graves and below tombstones greasy with moisture. On a low tomb with its top shaped like a roof, a round, grisly relic of the Mexican War gleamed darkly — the very cannonball that had killed the man who lay beneath it, a souvenir carefully retrieved at Veracruz and brought home with his shattered body to mark his grave forever. For the first time, really, I was oppressed by a sense of what a multitude of the dead were around us in that ancient burial ground, and how long some of them had lain there.

Where was that cheerful place where we had mowed and clipped the grass and snickered at Mitch's jingles about the Hawns and the Shedds — and the Duffs?

We walked along in silence, uneasily on the lookout for any sign of Ezekiel Zenger. Ahead of us, under the dismal trees, the outlines of the maintenance shed appeared, dour and forbidding, as though warning us to keep our distance. My feet began to drag. With very little encouragement I would have given up the whole idea of searching further for someone I did not expect to find, and might be afraid to look at if I did find him.

Ezekiel walked out of the shed.

What we felt then was like a jamming reversal of gears in a car. The sight of him brought us back to earth.

There he stood, as earthy and as real as ever. It was like looking through one of those stereopticon viewers, when everything is mixed up and hazy and hurts your eyes until suddenly they focus.

He stared at us with irritable surprise.

"What are you doing here?"

Fortunately we were still some distance away. Mitch had time to collect his wits and remember what it was he had planned to say.

"Hi, Mr. Zenger." His voice did a little fluting up and down the scale, as if it had not yet changed, but he managed to say his piece. "We thought we'd better come over and find out if you wanted us to work today."

The excuse got us by. Ezekiel looked almost approving, though he still delivered an impatient snort accompanied by a swift, professional glare up at the unaccommodating skies.

"Not if it stays like this," he snapped. But then

he found his way to the traditional New England brand of cautious optimism. "Still, it may burn off, and if it does . . . Well, you'll just have to keep an eye out. If we get some sun in an hour or so, we may be able to work."

"Okay, Mr. Zenger. If it burns off we'll check with you later."

Ezekiel gave us a brief nod.

"If we can work, I'll need you, because if I know Barney he probably won't show up at all today," he said bitterly, and dismissed us by stepping back into the shed.

Beyond him, beyond where he had stood, the Zengers kept their silent vigil in the graveyard where we had watched the last two members of the family behave so malevolently the day before. There, under the huge old trees that surrounded it, the shadows seemed deepest and blackest. Over on the Duff mausoleum the dark angel gleamed in the damp.

"Let's go," said Mitch.

I needed no urging.

Chapter 8

The Bradford house was one of the oldest in town. A guidebook described it as "an outstanding example of New England Colonial architecture." Its clapboards were painted white, its shutters black, and it was larger than it looked from the front because of the rambling additions that had been added from time to time long ago. When it was built, the whole neighborhood was Bradford farmland, right over to the boundaries of what was now the cemetery but had once been Zenger farmland.

The latest addition to the house, some fifty or sixty years ago, had been a front porch, but Mrs. Bradford had had it removed a few years back in order to restore the original lines of the house. History meant more to her than outdoor comfort.

Her quick footsteps, a small person's short strides,

clicked toward the front door before we had even rung the bell.

"I saw you coming," she said as she swung open the door.

The house was as much of a period piece inside as out. All the furniture was Early American, and so were the stiff family portraits on the walls of the low-beamed parlor. All the house needed was a few tasseled cords across doorways and it could have been a museum — except for one thing: the clutter.

Everywhere there was evidence of Mrs. Bradford's many activities. The Handicrafts Club, the Art Club, the Sewing Circle, and the Historical Society all contributed their bit in the way of original ceramics, a half-finished watercolor on an easel, embroidery frames with work in progress, and stacks of books and magazines.

She cleared a sheaf of pamphlets off a small sofa and told us to sit down. She settled herself opposite us in a wing chair that was a trifle high for her, so that her short legs, crossed at the ankles, did not quite touch the rag rug below them. Her bright eyes studied us intently.

"Now, then," she said. "Tell me all about it."

Telling her all about it took quite a while, because Mitch had to keep going back to fill in details in answer to her questions. By the time he finished, she had gotten everything out of him there was to get. And then she went over a lot of it again, as though to make sure nothing had been missed.

"When you first got there, Ezekiel was trying to scrub something off the gravestone, you say."

"Yes, ma'am."

"But he hadn't been able to get it all off, because later you could still see the outlines of it."

"That's right."

"What color was the paint?"

"Red, it looked like."

"How large was the symbol?"

"Well, I guess about six inches high."

"How soon after you got there did Nathaniel appear?"

"Almost right away."

"Ezekiel was angry, and they had words."

"Yes, ma'am. Just what I told you."

"And then the thunder and lightning scared you, and when you looked again they were gone."

"Yes."

"And you didn't see either of them again."

"No."

"You went and looked at the gravestone and saw it was Micah Zenger's, the oldest one in their family plot, and after that you noticed how the angel on the Duff mausoleum was pointing straight at you."

"Yes."

She chuckled in an odd, hard way.

"Well, that was enough to scare the dickens out of anyone, even if you didn't know —"

"We did know," said Mitch, surprising her.

"What do you mean?"

Mitch told her Mr. Bird's story about how Dr. Roberts and Colonel Duff wanted to change "Burial ground" to "Cemetery," and how both died in strange and sudden ways. She looked at us almost pityingly.

"So you knew. How odd. There aren't many people left who remember that affair, though of course an old codger like George Bird would. Well, now. I think it's time I explained a little more of the Zengers' history to you."

Behind her, against the wall, stood a tall grandfather clock that had measured off a couple of centuries a second at a time. Its slow beat filled the silence as she paused. There was no question about it, she was thoroughly in her element and enjoying herself, but it was a dark sort of enjoyment tinged with a grim concern that was ominous and disquieting.

"To begin with," she said, "Zenger is not the real family name."

We stared at her, confused by such an unexpected statement.

"What I mean is," she went on, "the family took that name after they left Salem."

"Salem?"

"Salem, Massachusetts. Do you boys know anything about Salem?"

"Sure! That's where they hanged the witches!" I burst out. Even then I knew that much about New England's history — thanks to Mrs. Bradford herself as much as anyone, because as a member of the school board she had seen to it that Colonial history was studied in our public schools. I shot a triumphant glance at Mitch. Had I been right, there in the library, when I suggested —?

"That's right, Howie." Mrs. Bradford almost seemed to have read my mind. "Back in the 1690s the Puritans went on a witch-hunt, and the witch-hunt in Salem was the worst. A few hysterical girls — about your age, Mitch — started accusing people of being witches, and being in league with Satan, and for a while no one was safe. Five men and eight women were hanged. And then, when they finally came to their senses and realized what they had done, the people of Salem were filled with shame. The horror of it hung over the village for generations.

"One old man was even tortured to death — the only time in our history when torture was officially and publicly used. His name was Giles Cory, and he was tortured because he stood mute."

"He what?"

"Well, it's a bit complicated, but I'm sure you boys can understand. When Giles Cory was accused of witchcraft, he refused to answer to the charge. As long as a man kept silent, he could not be placed formally on trial. If he couldn't be placed on trial he couldn't be convicted. And if he wasn't convicted his property could not be taken away from him by the state.

"He was an old man, and he was determined to save his property for his family. So he stood mute. He refused to speak.

"Now, in England when a prisoner stood mute he

was tortured in order to make him speak and give evidence. A particularly dreadful kind of torture was used for that purpose. It had a French name — *peine forte et dure* — which means 'strong and hard punishment.'

"It was inflicted on Giles Cory.

"The old man was taken out into a field by the sheriff, and stretched out on his back, and rocks were piled on his chest, one at a time — large, heavy stones. Giles was a big, rugged, barrel-chested man, but even so everyone thought that after a while, when the weight began crushing his chest and breaking his bones one by one, it would become unendurable and he would give in and agree to testify in court. But he stood the torture to the end, and the story is that the only words he spoke were, 'More weight.' "

Both Mitch and I had lively imaginations. What with the experiences we had been undergoing lately, they were perhaps in even sharper working order than usual. I am sure we were both pretty pale by then, and I know my head began to swim as I pictured the horrible scene in that Salem field two and a half centuries ago. At any rate, Mrs. Bradford came out of her story-telling trance sufficiently to look at us with alarm and quickly tried to break the spell.

"I don't mean to upset you, boys, but I do want you to understand what a terrible thing was involved. Because one of the men who had the most to do with seeing to it that Giles Cory suffered such a dreadful fate was an ancestor of the family we're talking about — the man buried as Micah Zenger."

Chapter 9

The reprieve came none too soon. By swallowing a few times and sneaking in a couple of deep breaths I managed to pull myself together and not disgrace myself. By now Mitch was looking a little less pale around the gills, too. He caught the meaning of her last remark.

"You mean his name wasn't really Zenger."

"That's right."

"What was it?"

Mrs. Bradford pressed her lips together and gazed at us regretfully.

"It took me years to run it down, and even now I feel it's better not to reveal it. Not so long as any of the family are still alive."

"You mean, Zeke and Nathaniel."

She nodded, and added a practical consideration.

"They wouldn't be above taking me to court. They're still a contentious lot."

"But how come the family could move here and take another name without anyone knowing it?" asked Mitch. "My gosh, Salem can't be a hundred miles from here —"

"Which, in those days, was as good as a thousand. In fact, by today's standards there's no way to compare it. Do you have any idea how few people ever made such a journey? Communications were very poor. People knew little about what went on outside their own villages. They had all they could do to tend to their own affairs. Besides, the Zengers — I'll have to call them that — didn't come here directly from Salem."

"Where did they go?"

Mrs. Bradford's face grew sad, with the special sadness of a defeated historian.

"That is one thing I have never been able to establish, where they moved to and stayed for several years before they came here. Town clerks kept atrociously haphazard records in those days," she complained peevishly, as if she wanted to rap their collective blockheads with her knuckles, "especially in new settlements on the fringes of the wilderness, which is probably where they went.

"All I know is that finally, in 1697, they turned up here with money enough to buy some land and build a house, and that a year later the head of the family, Micah Zenger, died and was buried in the plot they set aside for a family graveyard."

Her brown eyes darkened as she paused.

"And even then," she went on, "even then, when they had been here only a year, some unpleasant stories were already circulating about Micah and his family."

By now we were both in good health again and listening eagerly.

"What kind of stories?"

"Well . . . One thing we can be proud of our state for — our colony, I should say, because of course it was then still a colony — is that all during that time our people kept their heads. There were no witchcraft trials here. No poor old woman was ever hanged as a witch in *this* colony.

"But oddly enough, one of the very families that had been involved in the Salem persecutions — though nobody knew it then — began to be suspected of unnatural doings. This guilty family, this family that had helped cause innocent men and women to be accused of witchcraft and executed — one by torture — began to arouse suspicions among persons, *here*.

"Nobody came right out with it, so far as I can discover, but certainly there were suspicions. Strange things happened. Strange things were observed. One or two persons who didn't get along with the Zengers died very suddenly, in odd ways. Nothing could be proved, but there were circumstances . . . And then Micah's own death caused a sensation."

We both sat forward.

"How?"

Mrs. Bradford's gaze went straight through us, as though she were looking at something far more distant than two wide-eyed boys, or anything else of the here and now.

"One morning Micah was found drowned in a pond, and nobody could understand how it happened. According to a letter written at the time, he looked frightful. And persons who were the most suspicious of the Zengers and had the most reason to dislike them went around making remarks about how witches were supposed to hate water."

"Witches?" Mitch picked up the word with a gasp, and did not dare look at me. "You mean, people thought he was a *witch?*"

Mrs. Bradford snapped out of it, brought to attention by a historian's concern for accuracy of terms.

"A warlock, or wizard," she corrected. "A male witch is called a warlock, or possibly a wizard. At any rate, his death *was* mysterious. And it was only one of a long line of mysterious and sudden deaths, both of the Zengers and their enemies, that have occurred since then, the most recent being those of Dr. Roberts and Colonel Duff."

Again, in the silence that fell in the room, I was conscious of the somber voice of the grandfather clock reminding us of the long years that had come and gone since the "Zengers" left Salem. And as if Mrs. Bradford had guessed my thoughts, she added:

"The family left Salem because their neighbors shunned them after the witch-hunt madness, especially those who had shown the courage not to give way to it. But their curse, their own madness, went with them."

Mitch was wide-eyed again.

"Their *madness?* You mean, the whole family —"

"No." Mrs. Bradford was firm on that point. "No. They are the most tragic family I've ever studied, but not because they were all mad — in fact, precisely because they were . . . well, half-mad.

"There were always two distinct strains in the family, warring with each other. Some of them were civic leaders who did all sorts of good, at least publicly — for example, John Zenger, who gave the town the land for Hemlock Hill Burial Ground. Yet he had a brother Daniel who was suspected of all sorts of horrible things, and who got away just before a posse of townspeople carrying torches came looking for him.

"They came through the cemetery, right past the Zenger graveyard, and knocked over a couple of gravestones on their way past just to show how fearless they were — naturally, most of them were the usual rabble who turn out for such doings. Not one of them would have dared walk past the Zenger graveyard alone at that time of night. At any rate, Daniel fled before they reached the house, and was never seen again. John Zenger came out to meet the mob, and that was all that kept them from setting fire to the house, I expect."

My imagination was busy again, seeing that procession of torchlights bobbing past the Zenger grave-

68

yard, and hearing the angry shouts of the men as they stopped to push over gravestones.

"What is more, I gather that it was fear of John Zenger, rather than any liking for him, that kept the mob at bay that night, in spite of all his public good works. None of the Zengers ever seem to have been likable persons, but always high-handed, arrogant, and unapproachable."

She waved a plump hand at us.

"Well, that will give you some idea of what the Zengers were like," she said. And with that preamble out of the way she at last approached the subject of our visit. "But now, let me see that drawing again."

Mitch produced it and handed it to her. She studied it, nodding her head as she did so.

"Yes. Yes. You've got it exactly."

Almost as if he were afraid to hear the answer, Mitch asked,

"What is it?"

Mrs. Bradford looked up with a queer, embattled expression in her eyes and replied in a level tone,

"It is the mark of Satan."

Like all good historians, Mrs. Bradford had a strong sense of the dramatic. She also had that passion for accuracy I have already noted. So immediately she qualified her statement.

"That is to say, it's one of several symbols used in the worship of Satan, in the Black Mass, and so on."

"The Black Mass? I've read about that somewhere, but I'm not sure what it is," said Mitch.

"Do you know what Mass is? It's the celebration of the Holy Communion, the holiest service of the Catholic church. Many Protestant churches celebrate Communion, too, but they don't use the term 'Mass.' "

She paused, as though selecting her words carefully for what was coming.

"The Black Mass is a horrid, blasphemous imitation of Holy Communion, full of nasty mumbo-jumbo and ugly rituals all involved with the worship of Satan. When Ezekiel said that to Nathaniel about 'you and your' somebodies, he probably suspected, or knew, that something of the sort was involved in the defacing of the gravestone."

"You mean, in this day and age? . . ."

"Certainly. There have always been Devil cults and I suppose there always will be. Satanism, black magic, witchcraft — these things never die out. They always have their followers."

Nothing was changed in the room where we were sitting, and yet I felt as if shadows had gathered around us. What was this dark and secret world we had stumbled into?

Mitch was struggling to keep his footing in the world we knew.

"That old guy, in his baggy overcoat? I can't believe it!"

"It may seem like nonsense," said Mrs. Bradford,

"but Nathaniel could be mixed up in it, and could consider himself to be a warlock, with special powers."

"He's crazy!"

"He's mad," she agreed. "But . . . Well, for the present, anyway, I wouldn't go around talking to anyone else about this."

"Don't worry! We haven't said a word about it at home, have we, Howie?"

"I'll say not!"

"I think that's best, boys. I can imagine how your mother would take it."

"So can we! But . . . what shall we do?"

"Are you going to work in the cemetery again?"

"Yes. We went over to see if Zeke would want us this afternoon. If the weather clears up some we'll work."

"I see. Well, Ezekiel isn't a pleasant person, but at least he's no Nathaniel. If you observe anything else that seems out of the way, I hope you'll let me know."

"We will."

And with that promise, we left Mrs. Bradford.

Chapter 10

By noon the sun was struggling to come out, and by half past twelve it had made it. A few minutes later we climbed the wall and crossed the cemetery to report to Ezekiel.

We had talked it all over on the way home from Mrs. Bradford's. We were more or less of the same mind about our situation.

On the one hand, it frightened us to think of being around Ezekiel, and maybe seeing Nathaniel again, now that we knew what we did about them and their family.

On the other hand, we were burning with curiosity to know more, to see what might develop in the conflict between them. Mitch was perhaps a bit more eager to endure Ezekiel for the sake of that knowledge than I was. Without Mitch there to prod me along, I might easily have found excuses to stay away.

When we reached the shed Ezekiel was there, carefully sharpening a long-handled spade. In the sunshine he looked a trifle less forbidding.

"It'll be another hour before the grass is dry enough to mow well," he declared. "You can't start work till two o'clock — and mind ye, I only pay for the time you work."

Mitch nodded.

"Where do you want us to start at two?"

"Start with the Birds."

"I know where they are," said Mitch, who had not wasted our walks back and forth. "Over beyond the Harrisons."

"That's right. And while you're over thataway, go down the slope past the Birds and do the Xaviers."

If anything showed how the atmosphere had changed for us, it was the fact that Mitch did not brighten up when he heard that name. An *X!* Yet he hardly reacted.

Not that he hadn't put the notebook in his hip pocket from force of habit before we left home.

"That'll take you quite a spell, but I want you to work till you're finished, because I'm shorthanded. Barney hasn't shown up, just like I knew he wouldn't," Ezekiel went on bitterly, "and right when I've got a special to do, too."

If it had been anyone else, we would have asked what he meant by "a special," but of course we didn't dare ask Ezekiel. We collected our equipment from the shed and said we'd start on over. He gave us one of his economical nods and went back to sharpening the spade.

"What did he mean by 'a special'?" I asked as soon as we had put a comfortable distance between him and us.

"Beats me," said Mitch. We simply were not thinking straight, or we might have guessed. "If we see Joe, we'll ask him."

"What'll we do till two o'clock?"

"Oh, I don't know. Look at some of the tombstones, I guess. Maybe I can find some funny inscriptions to copy off."

As a matter of fact, we sort of enjoyed our enforced leisure. It was a luxury to be able to do what we wanted without having to worry about Ezekiel's being on our tails. We stopped a couple of times to examine unusual items. One was a Navy commodore's tomb with a huge anchor carved in granite on top of it and attached to the iron links of a real anchor chain that ran down out of sight into an edge of the tomb.

"I hope it's not attached to his leg," said Mitch.

Another marker was shaped like a pyramid about five feet high. Mitch decided it was the grave of some small-time Egyptian who couldn't afford a big pyramid. He was beginning to feel more like himself again, and so was I.

We were walking along one of the roads again when we heard a car coming. Mitch pushed his lawn mower off into the grass at the side while we turned to watch it pass. It stopped, however, and we were surprised to see who was at the wheel.

"Well, hello again, boys!" said Mrs. Bradford. "When the sun came out I decided to come over and do a little research for a piece I'm writing. Don't tell me Ezekiel's already put you to work?"

Mitch explained our situation.

"Oh. Well, then, how would you like to see the tombstone of a man who died of fright from seeing a ghost?"

She asked her question in a cheery voice, and Mitch and I grinned at each other while she was parking her car and getting out. There is nothing like strong sunshine for making ghosts sound silly. Mitch parked his lawn mower beside her car and I left my clippers in the grass.

"I'm glad I wore my galoshes," said Mrs. Bradford. "You boys ought to have something on your feet, too."

"A little wet grass doesn't hurt sneakers any," said Mitch.

"Nor you, either, I suppose. Well, now, Mr. Ebenezer Pratt is over this way," she said, and led us cross-country between the Bassetts and the Flahertys. "It was back in 1843 when he stumbled into a friend's house one dark night gasping something about seeing a ghost, and fell dead at his friend's feet."

"Any connection with the Zengers?"

"There might have been, but no one could be sure."

Mitch glanced at her sharply.

"Do you believe in ghosts?"

Mrs. Bradford stopped, looking thoughtful. Again she seemed to be choosing her words carefully.

"I keep an open mind," she said finally. "I've certainly never seen one myself, and hope I never will, but it's surprising how many people take them seriously. In England, now, there are all sorts of houses with a ghost or two that show up from time to time, and over there an amazing number of people take them for granted. But then, some of the houses and castles are so old . . ."

Her brown eyes twinkled with an odd satisfaction behind her rimless glasses as she went on.

"For that matter, they turn up in this country, too, and in places you wouldn't expect. Take the United States Military Academy, for instance — West Point. You wouldn't expect a lot of hard-headed, no-nonsense military men to be troubled by ghosts, would you? And yet West Point has its ghost."

"You're kidding!"

"I'm not. A ghost wearing an old-fashioned military uniform has been seen in a certain room in one of the dormitories there by any number of cadets. The commandant finally had to declare the room off limits, and no cadet is ever allowed to live in it."

"That's the craziest thing I ever heard of!"

"It may seem crazy, but it's true. I was reading about it not long ago. One interesting thing was that the cadets who have seen the ghost all reported the same thing, that just before the ghost appeared the room became icy cold. The same phenomenon has been reported in other places."

"Those cadets must have been studying too hard," said Mitch, refusing to take it in.

Mrs. Bradford's eyes flickered.

"Maybe. But still, I keep an open mind. It makes a good story, anyway."

She located Ebenezer Pratt's tombstone and carefully copied off dates and the inscription near the bottom of the stone:

FELLED BY FOUL FORCES.

"Now *there's* alliteration for you, Howie!" said Mitch the poet, and repeated it, hitting the *f*s hard. "*F*elled by *f*oul *f*orces!"

When she had finished, Mrs. Bradford turned back to us.

"To tell you the truth, I hoped to kill two birds with one stone here," she admitted. "I hoped I'd run across you boys, because after you'd gone I recalled something else I meant to tell you."

"Oh? What's that?"

"The day after tomorrow — or that night, rather — is an important date in the witches' calendar. It's Midsummer Eve, or Saint John's Eve."

"Oh?" said Mitch. "What's special about it?"

She opened her notebook.

"I copied out what is said about it in a book I

have," she declared, and read: "It was thought that supernatural creatures convened on that night at a designated field, where they conducted rites and were imbued with fresh powers. Hence it was necessary to secure doors and windows and seal all openings in houses, since the witches might be anxious to experiment with their newly acquired powers on the inhabitants."

She closed her notebook with a snap.

"If Nathaniel considers himself a warlock, he is probably part of a coven of witches, and it may be they'll gather together on that night."

"A — what did you say?"

"A coven. That's what a group of witches is called."

Mitch stared almost scornfully.

"You think there may be other nuts around here who think they're witches?"

"I don't know. I'm just remembering what Ezekiel said, and wondering. In any event, if you should be around when Nathaniel turns up again, you might keep your ears open."

"Okay, we will," said Mitch, without much conviction.

"Good. You see . . . well, I certainly wouldn't want you boys to start acting like those hysterical girls in Salem, but if Nathaniel *is* getting out of hand, and maybe leading others into dangerous territory, it would be well to know about it and, hopefully, to expose him."

She and Mitch exchanged a long glance, and they seemed to reach a silent understanding. His scorn was gone, his face was serious, and he suddenly asked a question I had not expected.

"Aren't you afraid?"

The question might have surprised me, but it did not surprise her. She nodded.

"A little. And you be careful."

"We will."

Her small mouth suddenly trembled.

"I may be doing wrong," she murmured. "I should tell you to go home this minute and stay away from here, because I just *don't know* . . ."

Mitch's expression was as strange as hers now, but his jaw was set.

"We wouldn't go anyway," he declared.

Mrs. Bradford's eyes probed into us, first Mitch and then me.

"Well, let me know," she said, "if *anything* . . ."

"We will."

She turned without another word and walked slowly back toward her car. Her shoulders had sagged and rounded, and her step was slow, not at all like her usual brisk pace. She looked terribly tired.

Chapter 11

We had not stirred. Until she had driven off, giving us a brief wave, we did not move.

When her car had gone out of sight, I turned to Mitch.

"I think she's read too many old books!"

He glanced at me absently.

"Maybe. Just the same, she's really worried. She's scared, too, but she's not about to let it get her down."

"She looked down to me."

"She'll be all right."

Mitch shook himself, almost as though he were shaking off a spell.

"Well, come on. Don't let it get *you* down, either!" He punched me on the arm and laughed, clearing the air. "Listen, if we just do our work and keep our eyes open, without making a show of it, we won't get into any trouble. What about it? Are you game?"

Real adventures don't come along too often in a boy's life. I thought about it, and made a grumpy admission.

"I couldn't leave now if I wanted to!"

I suppose the forces of light and darkness are always at war, and both have powerful weapons. Sunshine, for example — it was remarkable what effect a couple of hours of hot, steady sunshine combined with down-to-earth work had on us.

By that time we were ourselves again, cracking jokes and feeling normal. No one came near us except birds, all kinds of birds, and if anything can make the world seem all right it is a bunch of silly birds fluttering around, arguing with each other, looking for something to eat.

"Well, there are birds and there are Birds, capital *B*," said Mitch. "I'll bet this is George Bird's family. You know, the man who told Dad that story. Bird. Bird," he added thoughtfully, and I knew he had recovered.

"How about Xavier?" I said, and sure enough his face lit up.

"Yes, how about that? An X! Hmm..."

Pretty soon he was chuckling, and then his notebook came out. I waited.

"Okay," I said when he had stopped scribbling. "Let's hear it."

Mitch struck a pose and read with flourishes:

Here lies the body of Xerxes Xavier;
Someone objected to Xerxes's behavior.

I laughed till I was practically hysterical. Why does something seem funnier than usual when there is a sense of danger involved?

And even while I was still laughing at that one, Mitch was busy scribbling again.

"I guess I'll have to give up alliteration this time . . ." he muttered.

"Why?"

"Well, I'll have to use his real name."

"Whose?"

"Wait . . ."

When he had finished scribbling, he read:

> *Here lies the body of Ebenezer Pratt;*
> *Saw a ghost, and that was that.*

Before we were through he even added the Birds to his collection in what I still think was one of his finest efforts because of its tricky rhyme:

> *Here lies the body of Benedict Bird — er —*
> *All that was left, that is, after the murder.*

We did not finish doing the Birds and the Xaviers till well after five o'clock, and still Ezekiel had never come near us.

"Well, I'm not going to wait around," decided Mitch. "Let's take our stuff to the shed and see if he's there."

By then a cloud bank had come up in the west and it was no longer nice and sunny. For that matter, we did not have daylight saving time in those days, so that five o'clock was later than it would be today. I was glad to call it quits and go put our stuff away so we could head for home.

When we reached the shed Joe Palermo was there cleaning grass out of a lawn mower. He warmed us with one of his welcome smiles. Mitch glanced around, saw no sign of the boss, but still lowered his voice as he asked,

"Where's Zeke?"

Joe looked at us with surprise.

"Don't you know? He's doing a special."

Mitch laughed.

"Oh, sure — we meant to ask you, what's a special?"

Joe kept on smiling, but it was not quite the same smile. Some of his approval of life was gone from it.

"He's digging a grave."

We took this in for a moment.

"Might have known," muttered Mitch.

"He always digs the graves personally himself."

"Oh."

Joe looked around to make sure we were alone.

"Funny thing about Zeke," he added in a troubled voice, "he acts like he gets a special kick out of digging a grave. Sings, laughs, all the time he's digging. It's kinda creepy."

"Where's he digging this grave?" asked Mitch.

"We ought to check in with him, so he'll know how long we worked."

"He won't pay us if we don't," I piped up, and Joe grinned.

"Well, you know where the Dawsons are?"

"Over by the Shermans?"

"Hey, you're learning fast! That's right."

"Okay. We'll go see him," said Mitch. And from the undertone of excitement in his voice I knew he was interested in more than just checking in with Ezekiel.

We walked across the cemetery in the direction of the river through dull afternoon shadows that were rapidly darkening.

Mitch was like a field general planning his attack.

"We'll go around under the ridge and come up from the other side. That way we can get close without his seeing us. I want to watch him at work before we interrupt him."

Mitch was not telling me anything I had not already guessed. I had been thinking along the same lines.

"We've got to mind our p's and q's, Mitch. Nathaniel may be around somewhere by now, too."

My reminder made Mitch's head turn sharply as he took a check around. It was getting toward the time of day when we had often seen Nathaniel taking his walk. I remembered the times we had watched him from our kitchen windows, and wondered how we had ever been able to joke about him so easily.

The road we were following dipped sharply toward the foot of the ridge Mitch had in mind. Off to our left the tidal river was corrugated with swirling currents as its flow grappled with an incoming tide. We walked quietly, not scuffing along the way we normally would have, and our eyes were busy. At the bottom of the road we turned off without a word and began to creep along below the ridge.

Above us a large marble mausoleum with SHERMAN carved into the entablature over the doors stood on the brow of the ridge. Mitch motioned for me to stop and whispered, "Wait here."

He climbed the slope on hands and tiptoes and dropped behind the mausoleum, then edged sideways and took a careful look around one side of the building. After a moment he glanced down at me and beckoned. I joined him, moving as carefully as he had.

"Ease over this way and you can see him," he whispered. "It's all right, he's got his back to us."

I could hear him now, and the sound was grotesque. It was grotesque to think of Ezekiel Zenger singing at all, but he was, in a harsh, tuneless voice. He was singing a hymn:

> *When ends life's transient dream,*
> *When death's cold, sullen stream*
> *Shall o'er me roll . . .*

It was a hymn I had often heard in church, but never had it sounded the way it did when Ezekiel sang it. In church those words had sounded gloomy enough, but the mocking zest he put into them made me shudder. He was better than waist deep in the grave, making good progress. His spade added to the mound of dirt beside him with almost clockwork regularity. When he reached the end of the stanza he was growling out, he broke into a rasping chuckle.

"Yes, indeed, Amelia Dawson, we'll make you nice and comfy," he mumbled almost gaily. "I mind the time you jawed at me because someone had took those flowers off your husband's grave, as if I had nothing better to do than stand guard over every blessed bunch of posies in the whole place, but you won't be jawing at me any more, so we'll let bygones be bygones, won't we?"

Mitch and I looked at each other, and Mitch whirled a finger around beside his temple. Then he turned to watch Ezekiel again, and suddenly his elbow dug into my ribs. He whispered two syllables out of the side of his mouth.

" 'Thaniel."

In the distance, walking slowly along one of the winding roads, Nathaniel had come into sight. The broad-brimmed hat and baggy overcoat looked the same, but he was moving less vigorously than usual, and he was using a staff to help himself along. We watched him approach and wondered if Ezekiel had noticed him yet.

The way his spade hesitated, just missing part of a beat before picking up its regular rhythm again, told us he had.

Nathaniel's parchment face looked more like a death's head than before, drawn and unhealthy, but his smile was as sardonic as ever when he walked over, almost tottering, and stopped beside the grave. Only then did Ezekiel stop work and lean on his spade to look up at his brother.

"Well, Nate, you're not looking well, not well at all," he said by way of greeting.

"You're looking fine, Zeke, as you always do when you're at your favorite pastime," Nathaniel retorted contemptuously, and glanced around them. "Who is it for?"

"Amelia Dawson."

"Good riddance," said Nathaniel, and Ezekiel said nothing, not wanting to agree with his brother, I suppose. Instead, he shook a thick, stubby finger up at him.

"Been wanting to see you, Nate."

"I'm touched to hear it, brother."

"Been wanting to tell you I know what night it is that's coming up day after tomorrow. I'll be keeping an eye out, and if I see anything going on I don't like you'll pay for it!"

Nathaniel's watery eyes glittered savagely, and his chuckle was just as savage.

"Oh, you needn't worry, brother. You can stay in your cottage with everything shut up tight and get a good night's sleep, for all of me. I won't be here."

"Maybe you won't," said Ezekiel, and made a hard joke out of it. "You don't look long for this world."

"Don't you worry about that," snapped Nathaniel

in a cranky voice that did not sound altogether confident. "I simply meant I'll be elsewhere. I'm going out to Nantucket tomorrow for a few days."

Mitch and I exchanged an interested glance at that point. Nantucket is an island well offshore to the south and east of Massachusetts. It was famous for whalemen in whaling days.

"Going to Nantucket? Again?" Ezekiel snorted disgustedly. "Mean to tell me you're going to plague that poor place with another of your gatherings?"

"It should be very interesting," said Nathaniel, smiling hideously but with a strange, lordly superiority.

"You don't look like you're up to the trip," jibed Ezekiel. "You look seasick green already. And I see you're getting about with a stick now."

He laughed then, and patted the handle of his spade as he spoke to it.

"Yessir, old friend, it looks like you and me will have some more work to do before long, and won't *that* be a joy?"

It was a terrible thing to say to a man's face, even a face like Nathaniel's, and his response was just as terrible. He pushed himself erect with his staff, his eyes red and blazing, and thrust his hand out palm down above Ezekiel's head in a way that was a frightful travesty of a benediction.

"You miserable clod, you will dig your own grave before ever you dig mine!"

But Ezekiel only guffawed.

"I can wait, brother," he declared. "I can wait!"

Chapter 12

Fury seemed to strengthen Nathaniel, enough at least so that he was able to turn and stride away back to the road without tottering, while striking the ground with his staff at each step as though he intended to summon up the spirits of the dead.

And now we had our own troubles, because Nathaniel was heading on down the road, down the way we had come.

Mitch whispered urgently in my ear.

"Move! He'll see us!"

We scrambled sideways along the slope, dived over the top of the ridge on the far side of the Sherman mausoleum, and flattened out on the grass. We waited. Finally Mitch took a cautious look.

"It's okay. He's gone around the bend."

Mitch's face, when he turned back to me, was not

as pale as Nathaniel's had been, but it was pale enough.

"I don't care if he *doesn't* pay us for all our time, I'm not going near Zeke now!"

That suited me. Money isn't everything. All I wanted to do was leave unobserved.

We slipped back down the slope and headed for home. At least, so I thought.

"You going to tell Mrs. Bradford about this, Mitch?"

"Sure."

"When?"

"Now."

"Now? We'll be late for supper."

"Not if we hurry."

We hurried.

Mrs. Bradford shook her head, horrified.

"It's dreadful," she said. "It's dreadful for two brothers to talk that way to each other."

Mitch had no time for moralizing, however.

"What about Nantucket?" he asked. "Do you know anything about that?"

She nodded.

"A little. I know there have been rumors."

"Rumors?"

"Rumors of such gatherings out there. An island, especially one that's fairly remote, is an attractive place, you know, for . . . There was a piece in the paper a few years ago reporting strange doings in a field out there on Midsummer Eve. Of course the paper had a lot of fun with it, and apparently nobody took it seriously — nobody here on the mainland, at least. I don't know how they felt about it out on Nantucket."

Then she brightened a little.

"Well, at least we won't have to worry about Hemlock Hill this year."

Mitch was immediately alert.

"Has anything gone on there in the past that you know of?"

"Nothing I know about firsthand. Again, only rumors."

Once more she looked worried, and seemed to come to a decision.

"But I don't like this," she declared. "I feel a responsibility, and I don't like it. I mustn't encourage you to take any more chances. I've been thinking about it, and . . ."

She faced us squarely.

"I want you to stop going over there."

Mitch stared at her.

"You mean, stop working there?"

"Yes."

He squirmed around in his chair, frowning.

"We're making good money," he pointed out.

"Well, make it somewhere else. Don't go back there."

Mitch sprang up and paced around. Then he stopped in front of Mrs. Bradford.

"I *can't* stop now," he said simply. "I'd go crazy,

wondering what was going on. Besides, Nathaniel won't even be around for the next few days, so what is there to worry about?"

She considered this, and was tempted. Certainly she was as eager as Mitch to know more, if more could be known.

"Well..."

"Why not? We can worry about quitting later. When Nathaniel comes back, we'll see."

But she shook her head at this.

"When Nathaniel comes back," she said firmly, "you quit."

"But —"

"You must. Really. If you don't, I'll have to speak to your parents."

Mitch was appalled.

"You mean, *tell* them —?"

"If you force me to. Mitch, you must be sensible. How do you think I would feel if . . . anything happened to you two?"

For a moment he met her eyes seriously. Then he grinned.

"Nobody would know you knew about us."

"*I* would know."

Mitch's eyes slid away uncertainly.

"Well..."

"Promise me."

He struggled with himself, obviously thinking about all that money he would be giving up. Finally he shrugged.

"Well, okay. Let's see how it goes..."

"No." Mrs. Bradford's voice rang out in the cluttered old Colonial room. "When Nathaniel returns, I want you to quit."

By the time we left, Mitch had agreed.

The next day the sun was really on the job again, beaming down from a cloudless sky. As we crossed toward the shed, the cemetery had never looked more normal, even cheerful, with a feeling of life everywhere, in the grass and the trees and the flowers, in the birds and the squirrels and the butterflies.

From a high point along the way we could see the Dawson plot. The new grave was a mound now, covered with a blanket of flowers. The funeral services had been held that morning.

When the shed came into sight, Joe was outside, alone, busy cleaning out some flowerpots.

"I hope Joe can tell us where we're supposed to work today, so we won't have to talk to Zeke," said Mitch. "It won't be easy to act natural around Zeke, so far as I'm concerned."

When we reached the shed, however, Ezekiel appeared, spoiling our hopes. He stared at us, and I wondered how he would have looked if he knew we had watched him and his brother last evening.

"How long did you boys work yesterday?"

Mitch told him.

"That's right," said Joe, and Ezekiel nodded. Joe seemed to be one of the few persons he respected.

"All right, I'll note it down. Now, today there's

a whole section of small plots I want you to do," he said, and told us where they were. Past the Hawns, to the right of the Gilhooleys, then draw a bead on the Gregorians and our section was in between.

We found it with no trouble. And while we worked we talked about Ezekiel.

"It was hard to look at him today and still believe he could have acted the way we saw him acting yesterday," said Mitch. "He seems back to normal."

"Not that normal is anything to brag about," I pointed out. "I'll say one thing, he's got the worst singing voice I ever heard."

"Worse than Miss Farthingale," agreed Mitch, mentioning one of our church choir's shrillest sopranos. "Next time he digs a grave I don't think I'll attend the ceremony."

We clipped and mowed for a while, and then Mitch said, "I wonder how Nathaniel is doing out on Nantucket."

"I wonder how Nantucket is doing."

"I'm almost sorry he went," Mitch added perversely. "I'd like to have seen what might have gone on here."

I stared up at him.

"Don't tell me you'd come over here to snoop around tomorrow night!"

The poet's curiosity was afire again.

"I just might have."

"Huh! Not me! There isn't *anything* could get me over here tomorrow night!"

I meant it.

Before we finished work Mitch had perked up enough to need his notebook again. One of the families we were doing that day was named Yost, so Mitch added *Y* to his roster:

Here lies the body of Yolanda Yost;
Some of it came back by parcel post.

We took our equipment to the shed and walked home under skies that were cloudless and sunny.

Chapter 13

The next morning when we came to breakfast Dad was reading the morning paper. He looked up over it and said,

"Say, here's something that will interest you boys. You know that old fellow we've seen walking around over in the cemetery, Nathaniel Zenger?"

Mitch was moving his chair out, about to sit down at the table. He stopped, one hand gripping the back of the chair.

"Sure, Dad. What about him?"

"Well, it seems he died last night, out on Nantucket."

Dad's expression of mild interest changed when he saw how pale we both became. And of course Mom's expression did more than that.

"Why, what's the matter, boys?" she cried, ready to jump up and start feeling foreheads.

"Don't tell me you've gotten to know him over there?" asked Dad.

Mitch made an effort to recover himself. He dropped into his chair and said, "Well, no, but we've seen him around a couple of times, and —"

"He didn't look so hot the last time we saw him," I added, and Mitch nodded without glancing at me.

"Well, you don't have to feel too bad," said Dad. "He was eighty-seven."

Mitch nodded absently.

"It's hard to believe, though," he said. "Does it say anything about, uh, how . . . ?"

"No, it just says he died suddenly. I wonder what he was doing out on Nantucket? I guess he must have some friends out there. At least, the paper says some friends of his there have chartered a small plane to bring the body home. It's to be flown over this afternoon. Funny, though. Not many men that age go jaunting off to visit friends. Not many have any friends left to visit."

Mitch asked for the paper and read the news item.

"Funeral services will be held tomorrow," he muttered, and our eyes met across the table as the same grisly thought struck both of us. The special of specials would soon be under way.

When we climbed over the wall that afternoon, the fine weather was gone again. High clouds were taking over, streaky and mean-looking.

"Yesterday should have been Midsummer Day," said Mitch, recalling its perfection.

"Midsummer Day's tomorrow."

"Oh, that's right."

Ezekiel was very much on our minds.

"I don't suppose he reads the papers, and he doesn't even have electricity in his cottage, from what Joe says, so he can't listen to the radio. Still, someone is sure to have notified him," Mitch decided as we hurried along in sickly sunshine that was rapidly giving up the game. "After all, he's next of kin — the only kin left, for that matter."

"I'm glad I didn't have to tell him. I wonder how he acted?"

"I'll bet he didn't pretend to shed any tears."

I looked over in the direction of the Dawson plot. The blanket of flowers, beautiful yesterday, was faded and dead. It looked as bygone and pathetic as some worn-out old crazy quilt.

"I wonder if he's dug the grave yet," I muttered.

I thought about the small plane that was going to bring the body home. Only the pilot would be accompanying it, the newspaper had said.

"Funny to think of Nathaniel flying . . ."

"Beats a broomstick," said Mitch with a thin grin.

"I wouldn't want to be that pilot."

When we reached the shed nobody was in sight. We hardly looked toward it, though. Our eyes went past the shed, watching for the Zenger graveyard to come into sight under the trees. When it did, our footsteps faltered and stopped.

"Look at that," breathed Mitch. "Listen!"

99

Over in the Zenger graveyard, shoulder deep in the ground, Ezekiel was digging and singing:

And such the trust that still were mine
Though stormy winds swept o'er the brine,
Or though the tempest's fiery breath
Roused me from sleep to wreck and death.
In ocean cave still safe with thee
The gem of immortality!
And calm and peaceful shall I sleep
Rocked in the cradle of the deep.

The gusto with which Ezekiel was singing now made his performance of the other day seem subdued.

"What'll we do, Mitch?" I asked.

He hesitated for only a second or two.

"Well, we've got to find out where we're supposed to work."

He took a deep breath and started over, straight toward where Ezekiel was doing his special of specials. I tagged along, a walking cluster of goosepimples. When we were near, Ezekiel noticed us out of the corner of his eye. He stopped singing and turned to face us. His earth-colored face was sickeningly merry.

"That there is one of my favorite tunes. Been running through my head all day," he said. "Well, boys! Heard the news? I've lost my only flesh and blood!"

"Yes, sir, we heard," said Mitch.

Ezekiel slapped a hard palm flat on the turf beside him and made a sound that was like a triumphant gurgle.

"Told me I'd dig my own grave before ever I dug his, he did — but he was wrong!"

The temptation for Mitch to say "we know" was great, but you can be sure he didn't say it. Instead he said,

"Yes, sir. Er — where do you want us to work today?"

Ezekiel waved his hand expansively, like a man on holiday.

"Oh, I don't know . . . Lemme see, now . . . Guess you might as well tend to the Biggerstaffs. They could stand it. Know where they are?"

"Yes, sir. Over that way," said Mitch, pointing.

"Kee-rect! Well, you skedaddle over thataway, and mebbe I'll be over later when I've finished here. Clear away all that ragged growth around the base of the shaft, now, and make it look real pretty."

Ezekiel was normally a trial, but a jocular Ezekiel, an Ezekiel in high spirits, was hard to bear. We hurriedly fetched our equipment from the shed and took off for the Biggerstaffs, who fortunately lay a good distance from the Zengers, well out of earshot.

It was a long afternoon, and a dreary one. Under high, scudding, iron-gray clouds a stiff, variable wind seemed to change its quarter every few minutes.

"Getting ready for Midsummer Eve," Mitch grumbled.

I tried to make a joke — "It won't be the same without Nathaniel" — but Mitch didn't laugh, and neither did I. His notebook never appeared that afternoon, either. We simply worked hard, and looked over our shoulders from time to time to see if Ezekiel was coming, hoping he wouldn't. But then, just as we were finishing, he showed up, stumping along across the grass in his dusty boots with a step that was almost jaunty.

He inspected our work and nodded.

"It'll do. Trim up a mite more over there around the Benjamins and then call it a day. That's what I'm going to do. I'm going home now and enjoy myself!"

Having made this astounding statement he nodded again and left us. We took care of the final touches he had ordered and made tracks for the shed.

"What about the funeral tomorrow, Mitch?"

"I'm going."

"Maybe it'll be in the afternoon when we have to work."

"I'll go anyway. And if Zeke says anything, I'll quit then and there."

The poet's jaw was set.

"I want to see that funeral!"

Chapter 14

It was Midsummer Eve. Saint John's Eve. Mitch and I were the only ones in our house who knew it, though. All our parents knew was that it was Friday night and they were going to have their regular Friday night game of bridge with the Wilsons, over at their house.

They did not leave till seven-thirty. After seven-thirty, in fact, because Dad wanted to hear the news on the radio. When they were ready to leave, he came by our room.

"Say, that plane that's bringing old Zenger back hasn't turned up at the airport yet, and it was reported as leaving Nantucket in the middle of the afternoon," he said. "They're worried, because there was a terrific thunderstorm out at sea a while ago. Several boats are out looking around."

Mitch stared up at Dad for a moment. Then he reached across his desk and turned on the radio he had built himself.

"Thanks for telling us, Dad. We'll listen in and see if there's any more news about it."

"Are you going anywhere tonight, Mitch?" asked Mom. If he wasn't going to a movie, he sometimes went over to some friend's house for a while, and sometimes I went, too, if he was in the mood to let me tag along, or if there was a younger brother my age where he was going.

"No, I don't think so, Mom," he said. "I guess we'll be right here."

They left for their bridge game, which was a relief. I felt as if I'd been holding my face in one position for about a month. We could hardly wait to talk about the news. As soon as they were gone we both let out a big breath and Mitch jumped up to pace around.

"What's going on?" he cried in a queer, edgy voice.

"What do you mean? I guess there was a big storm and —"

"It's weird," he muttered, ignoring me. "It's all weird . . ."

He paced some more, then swung around and spoke again in the same edgy voice.

"Remember that hymn Zeke was singing? The one he said had been running through his head all day?"

I remembered then, and the memory jarred me.

"Rocked in the cradle of the deep!"

It had certainly bored into Mitch's mind, because he repeated part of it word for word:

And such the trust that still were mine
Though stormy winds swept o'er the brine,
Or though the tempest's fiery breath
Roused me from sleep to wreck or death . . .

His voice shook with dark excitement.

"But that was *before* the plane went down, before it had even left Nantucket! I tell you, it's weird. It's all very, very weird . . ."

In my mind I could hear Ezekiel singing again, singing those words, and they made my flesh crawl. I glanced out the window at the trees that were whipping around under a patchwork sky.

"I suppose we ought to get all the doors and windows closed," I said, and tried to carry it off with a snicker.

"Oh, shut up," snapped Mitch, and sat down to fiddle with the radio.

Time dragged by, because neither of us could settle down to anything. There was nothing on the radio but a bunch of boring junk, but we had to listen.

"They might break in anytime with a news flash if . . ."

At eight o'clock Mitch found a station that gave a

brief newscast, but the announcer only repeated what Dad had told us earlier. By then the big stations were into their prime-time programs — in those days, long before television, radio was king. Mitch checked the paper and said there wouldn't be any more regular news programs till ten o'clock.

While we fidgeted more minutes passed, but they passed like pallbearers. Outside it grew darker and darker, while the wind lashed the trees and rattled the windows in their casements. Finally Mitch got up and shut both windows tight. We listened irritably to a radio play that was not worth the paper it was written on.

"Why don't they forget this hooey and give us some news?"

At last the play ended and there was a station break.

"One more hour. One more hour and then maybe we'll know something."

Again Mitch consulted the newspaper, and reached for the tuning dial.

"Well, at least there's a little better program coming up —"

"We interrupt to bring you a special news bulletin," said the local announcer. "Wreckage of a small plane has been sighted at sea, approximately twelve miles off New Bedford. It is believed to be the plane that was carrying the body of Nathaniel Zenger of this city, who died last night at Siasconset on Nantucket Island. To repeat," said the announcer, and repeated the news item, then returned the station to the national network.

Until the announcer did that, neither of us moved. We simply listened, stared at each other, and listened again.

Then, with a shaking hand, Mitch turned off the radio. The sudden quiet was like a silent explosion.

He was staring at me again, or through me would be more accurate, and he looked feverish. I could see something growing in him, some crazy idea.

"Zeke," he said suddenly. "What on earth will Zeke say when he hears about *this?*"

His eyes focused on me with a wild resolve.

"I'm going to tell him."

I jumped about a foot in my chair.

"What?"

"He doesn't have a radio. He won't know."

"But *somebody* will go —"

"Who? Why? How many people know he doesn't have electricity? And how many will give a darn if they *do* know? Who else is going to bother to go to a cemetery at this time of night just to tell Zeke Zenger his brother's body has been lost at sea in a plane crash?"

"A reporter, maybe."

Mitch started as if I had pinched him.

"Say, that's right! Still, if one of those guys does come out here he'll have to climb the wall and walk over to Zeke's place, because the gates are closed and locked."

Have you ever had an older brother who you thought had suddenly lost his marbles? That was the way I felt when Mitch jumped to his feet and said,

"I'm going to get there before *they* do!"

I goggled up at him, absolutely speechless. And he picked that instant to act reasonable!

"Well, *somebody* ought to tell him," he said, "and if I don't, maybe nobody else will!"

The worst of it was, his fever was catching. When I looked out the window at that dark night, and at those trees hammering the air, I could feel myself shrink. But when I thought about Ezekiel, and began to wonder how he *would* take the news . . . And after all, whatever he did, there was no reason to think he would hurt us, or anything like that.

So . . .

Chapter 15

If anyone had told me I would run across Hemlock Hill Burial Ground on a wild Midsummer Eve — and believe me, we ran — I would have said he was crazier than either Zenger brother, even crazier than *my* brother. Hadn't I said only yesterday there wasn't *anything* that could have gotten me over there that night?

Yet there I was, pounding along beside Mitch.

One thing I had not realized, looking out under the trees from our windows, was that the darkness was not as complete as I had thought. That was why we were able to run full tilt.

The wind had torn jagged shreds in the clouds, and behind them, seeming to scud along, a gibbous moon shone like a pale wraith from time to time. As strong as the wind was, it was warm, almost sticky warm, so that sweat was soon running down our faces.

We could see where we were going, but I almost wished we couldn't. Total darkness might have been better. The flaring, fleeting moonlight made everything look unfamiliar. Tall cenotaphs shone lividly and then disappeared. Tombs loomed up like monsters and then faded away. Rows of gravestones gleamed like dragons' teeth one moment and were gone the next. As to what might be behind us, I never dared glance back to learn, but always, all the way across that horridly transformed place, I felt I had better run as fast as I could, because if ever I stopped, or staggered, or fell . . .

We kept going. And finally we could see the Duff mausoleum ahead of us, with something massive and shadowy on top of it, and beyond the mausoleum the shed, and beyond that . . .

"Where *is* his cottage?"

"It's got to be close to — It's over there beyond the — beyond their — Come on!"

It was not bad enough to be there at all — now we had to run straight past the Zenger graveyard, with that open grave waiting for a body that had not been recovered. A body that was probably in a casket at the bottom of the Atlantic Ocean by now. I couldn't close my eyes and still run, but I certainly kept them straight ahead as we went past. Or anyway, I tried. I tried, but not quite enough to keep myself from catching one terrible glimpse of a black rectangle in the turf as we went by.

"There!"

Ahead of us in a small clearing we could see a dim

glow of light. It had to be a kerosene lantern in Ezekiel's cottage. I told myself it had to be that.

And it was. The outlines of a cottage gradually stood out in the darkness, especially when the moon slid from behind the clouds for brief instants, and I was surprised to see that, though small, it was a two-story affair, tall and narrow rather than low and spread out.

The glow of the lantern came from the second floor.

But now, as we pulled up a few yards from the cottage, Mitch was finding that it was one thing to talk about telling Ezekiel the news and another thing to walk up to the door and do it. He shuffled to a stop and glanced at me, and even in the darkness I could see the whites of his eyes, all of them.

Then, as we hesitated, terror took over.

All at once the air grew icy cold, as though the coldest wind we had ever felt was sweeping past us — yet every leaf around us was suddenly still. The deathly chill of it went straight to the bone and made my tongue cleave to the roof of my mouth.

For an instant, while our teeth chattered and our bodies shivered, even though the cold had passed on as quickly as it had come, there was silence.

Then a choking voice cried out in the cottage. Ezekiel's voice.

"*You!* No! You f-foul —"

Words blurred into a strangled gasp, and then the cottage shook, as though something heavy had fallen to the floor. As though a mountain had fallen.

Once more a wind was blowing, but now it was warm again, and the leaves had gone back to their mad dance. Before I could even think about moving, Mitch had stepped forward.

"Where are you going?" I cried in a shrill voice, too scared to hold it down.

He looked around at me with wild eyes.

"We can't just go away now! We've *got* to see if Zeke —"

"We can't go in there! Someone else must be —"

"No one else is there." Mitch spoke with inexplicable assurance.

"But we *can't* —"

"We've got to!"

It was the same old story. Mitch had to *know*. He could not stop now until he knew what had happened. He was walking forward on stiff legs toward the door of the cottage.

And by some miracle I found myself following him. For all the feeling there was in them my legs might have been missing altogether, and yet they moved me forward.

The door of the cottage stood ajar. A dim glow from the lamp upstairs showed a narrow crack between its edge and the door jamb. From inside the cottage came not a sound.

Slowly, making a tremendous effort of will, Mitch reached out a hand and touched the door.

With only the slightest of creaks it swung open in an unhurried arc and bumped gently once, twice against the wall as it stopped.

Straight ahead of us across a cramped entry a steep and narrow flight of stairs ran straight up to the second floor. Lamplight from a room at the top picked out the edges of the treads.

Mitch wiped a fist across his lips, then called out in a voice that was little more than a dry whisper.

"Mr. Zenger?"

There was no answer.

"Mr. Zenger!"

Still no answer.

Walking like a zombie, as though some will other than his own were keeping him going, he stepped inside. And I had gone too far now to draw back alone. Together we started up the steep, narrow stairs. There was just room enough for us, side by side. Two, three, four, five steps, and then we could look into the room at floor level.

We could see only part of the room, but we could see enough.

Ezekiel's legs, the broad toes of his dusty boots turned up, stretched into sight on the floor. Above them lamplight caught the rectangle of a window, its glass frosted as though it were midwinter instead of midsummer. And in the frost was etched the symbol.

For a moment as endless as it was brief we stared at the rigid legs and that evil symbol that seemed to flicker and glow on the window above them. Then icy cold air rushed down toward us, icy, freezing cold.

We turned and fled, stumbling down the stairs,

bursting through the doorway, pounding away off into the night. We ran blindly, seeing nothing, wanting only to get away, and there is no telling how far we might have gone had I not stubbed my toe on a boundary marker near the Duff mausoleum and gone sprawling.

Mitch stopped then and rushed back to me, ducking down beside me like a soldier under fire.

"Howie!"

One thing saved me from dissolving into gibbering panic. I felt an overwhelming sensation of dark wings stretched over us, shielding and protecting us. And I could feel blood on a knee, and that was somehow reassuring.

"I'm okay," I said.

"Then come on. We've got to call the cops and tell them about Zeke!"

But then I raised my head and stared back the way we had come, and my heart was in my throat again.

"Mitch! Look!"

A string of dim, wavering lights was glimmering and bobbing under the trees beside the Zenger graveyard, like spectral torchlights. Even as we looked they disappeared. And before either of us could speak, a beam of light swept across the base of the trees.

We heard a motor. The beam appeared again, stronger now, and over beyond the trees, on a road.

"Sweeney! I never thought of him!" said Mitch.

Officer Sweeney was the cemetery policeman. He checked around in his prowl car every night before closing time, and was in charge of shutting and locking the gates at sunset.

"He's come to tell Zeke!"

We stared into the night, waiting, thinking about what Officer Sweeney had in store for him.

"Mitch," I said after a moment. "Was that his headlights?"

"Had to be!"

"But he didn't come from that direction."

Mitch looked at me, and looked away. We heard the prowl car stop. We waited. My chest ached from holding my breath without knowing it. Then a car door slammed and an engine was gunned. The headlights swung in a wild arc under the trees, almost reaching the base of the Duff mausoleum beside us, and Officer Sweeney's prowl car roared back along the road.

"He'll go to the office and call an ambulance," Mitch said. In those days there were no radio phones in police cars, at least not in those of special policemen like Officer Sweeney.

Say what you will, there is nothing like having a policeman around to give you courage. It helped Mitch. It gave him the courage for one last effort.

"Listen," he said. "You wait right here."

"Why?"

"There's something I want to do."

"What?"

"I want to go back over there for a minute."

"*What?*"

"Just for a second."

"Are you nuts?"

"I'll be right back."

"But *why?*"

"There's something I want to see."

"Aw, Mitch!" I squawked, but he was already walking away, back toward the cottage. I scrambled to my feet and limped after him. "Listen, I'm not going to sit here alone —!"

"Then come on."

Maybe I was in a state of shock. At any rate, somehow I managed to pad along behind Mitch all the way back to the cottage, all the way past that Zenger graveyard with its open grave, until finally we were standing in front of the cottage door again.

Officer Sweeney had left it open wide.

"Okay!" I said then, "what do you want to see?"

"The window," said Mitch, and went in.

We mounted a few steps, just enough to see the window.

It was a black, gleaming sheet of glass in the lamplight, without a mark on it, or any frost.

Chapter 16

So that was how Ezekiel Zenger happened to dig his own grave without knowing it, and how we found ourselves attending his funeral instead of his brother Nathaniel's.

When our parents came home from their bridge game that Midsummer Eve they had heard the news — by then even the news of Ezekiel's death had come over the radio — so they were not surprised that we seemed worked up about it. We let it go at that.

We went to see Mrs. Bradford the next morning and told her the whole story. It was a comfort to know one person who would believe us, who would take it seriously.

"The papers say Zeke apparently died from a heart attack," said Mitch.

"I know. And we had best leave the matter there," said Mrs. Bradford. She studied us with deep interest.

"I'm struck by the fact that you had that sudden sensation of icy coldness just before, and after . . . You both felt it?"

"Yes."

"And you both saw the frost on the window, and the symbol marked in it?"

"Yes."

Mrs. Bradford could not control a shudder. She was plainly shaken.

"I don't know what to think about it — but I believe you. I simply hope this is the last of it."

We were all in agreement there.

Needless to say, because of the bizarre circumstances surrounding the deaths of both brothers, there were more persons at Ezekiel's funeral services than might otherwise have attended, and they all came along from the cemetery chapel to see him lowered into the grave he had dug himself.

The minister said the words of the burial service, the graveside words about ashes to ashes and dust to dust, rather more briskly than he might otherwise have done, because the skies were threatening and it looked as if we might get a thunderstorm at any moment. Mrs. Bradford was there, of course, and we glanced at each other from time to time.

I found myself thinking about Mitch's jingles — "Here lies the body" — and I knew that now he would never complete the alphabet. Certainly he would never get to Z. "Here lies the body of Ezekiel

Zenger . . ." No. He would never write that one. And he would never read any of them aloud at home to our parents.

When the coffin had been lowered into the grave, the minister walked slowly away and the crowd drifted after him, but we stayed to watch while Joe and Barney — yes, Barney! — shoveled earth into the rectangular pit above the coffin until it was mounded up in a fashion that would have satisfied Ezekiel.

Then they shouldered their spades and trudged away toward the maintenance shed, and we turned away, too, heading for home. I tried to keep my eyes away from the dark figure atop the Duff mausoleum, pointing its unwavering finger at the last of the Zengers.

We were passing the mausoleum when suddenly we were chilled to the bone. An icy coldness swept past us, making us stop and turn and stare back the way we had come. And then Mitch grabbed my arm.

A dust devil was swirling around in the dirt on top of the grave. As we watched it thickened and rose and took on vague outlines, billowing out the way a coat might have done. It lasted only a moment, then whirled away and disappeared.

Mitch let go my arm and started running, back toward the grave, and I followed.

When we reached the grave we looked down and saw, for the third time, the clear outlines — etched in the dusty earth on top of the grave — the outlines of that awful symbol.

Lightning flashed, a clap of thunder split the air, and the heavens opened. We were soaked within seconds, but we hardly knew it as we watched the rain beat the earth into a blank, shiny slick of mud.